THE SECRET PACT

A Novel by

John W. Gemmer

CCB Publishing
British Columbia, Canada

The Secret Pact: A Novel

Copyright ©2020 by John W. Gemmer
ISBN-13   978-1-77143-427-0
First Edition

Library and Archives Canada Cataloguing in Publication
Title: The secret pact / a novel by John W. Gemmer.
Names: Gemmer, John W., 1948- author.
Identifiers: Canadiana (print) 20200282662 | Canadiana (ebook) 20200282697 |
ISBN 9781771434270 (softcover) | ISBN 9781771434287 (PDF)
Classification: LCC PS3607.E55 S43 2020 | DDC 813/.6—dc23

Cover design by Donika Mishineva: website: www.artofdonika.com

Publisher: CCB Publishing
             British Columbia, Canada
             www.ccbpublishing.com

Dedication

This book is being dedicated to my significant other and best friend, Hope Anna Heritz.

Acknowledgements

Thanks to Kevin Sheets, Bill Abshire, Alicia Rasley, and Hope, for their help and encouragement. Special thanks also to Jeff Rasley, my very talented editor, and Paul Rabinovitch, my publisher, CCB Publishing, British Columbia, Canada. Without their help I would not have been able to complete this book to my satisfaction.

Books by John W. Gemmer

The Last Assignment

Harsh Consequences

Terrorists in the Heartland

Evil Lives Among Us

The Secret Pact

Preface

How far will he go to win? Who can he trust? Who will assist him and who will try to stop him? Those are the questions David Weiss, star athlete, brilliant businessman, husband, father, and possible murderer must answer.

In the second book of Plato's Republic Socrates argues that most people are fundamentally self-interested, yet they try to convince others that they are virtuous and just. Those too weak to live by principles of justice and virtue will behave hypocritically in a fruitless endeavor to gain a good reputation within their community. While the bold but unjust man, who is cunning enough to fool others, will prevail over weaker and lesser men. While only he who truly loves the Good, the True, and the Beautiful will have the personal fortitude to live a virtuous life.

Socrates goes on to describe the mythical Ring of Gyges, which gives the owner the power of invisibility. If a man obtained the Ring, his unjust actions could be hidden and only his just actions revealed. Such a man would never have to fear the consequences of his unjust actions. And those who know he owns the magical ring will fear him, but they will never trust him.

THE SECRET PACT

Chapter 1

Albert C. Weiss' relatives lived in the southern part of Germany for centuries, primarily in the Munich area. Many in the Weiss family became well-known, prosperous, and respected members of their communities. The Weisses were particularly successful in retail and financial enterprises.

By the time the First World War ended on November 11, 1918, a few Weiss family members from the Munich area, were already well-established in the United States. But not all of the Weisses were involved in legitimate businesses. Some were involved in criminal activities such as bootlegging, loan-sharking, gambling, and bookmaking. They had amassed fortunes from their criminal activities.

When Prohibition ended in the United States in 1933, some members of the Jewish mob, who made fortunes illegally selling alcohol, left the criminal life behind to invest in legitimate industries, like the media and entertainment, precious metals and jewelry, textiles, and finance. Even some of the most notorious members of the Jewish mob, such as those connected to the infamous gangster Arnold Rothstein, became legitimate businessmen. However, long-time family and business relationships with gangsters in the Jewish and Italian mobs did not all end with the end of Prohibition.

In the early 1930's, a small number of affluent and forward-thinking Weisses, including Albert C. Weiss, sold their businesses and left Germany. They departed their beloved Deutschland aboard German ships, like the M.S. St. Louis, bound for the United States. Those Weisses, along with increasing numbers of other Jewish families, left their homeland because of the discrimination Jews began to experience when the National Socialist German Workers' Party, also known as the Nazis, gained power. The Jews who left Germany in the early 1930's rightly anticipated matters would get much worse for Jews under the Nazis. Several of the Weisses who had previously immigrated to the United States from Germany lived in the New York City area. They helped members of the extended Weiss family, who escaped Nazi oppression, to obtain legal entry into the US.

Other members of the greater Weiss family, who couldn't afford the costs of immigrating to the United States, managed to leave Germany and relocate to France, Belgium, the Netherlands, Denmark, Czechoslovakia, and Switzerland. By the summer of 1938, most of the Weisses had left Germany. When Kristallnacht (Night of the Broken Glass) occurred throughout Germany on November 9-10, 1938, it was evident to most German Jews that they were in serious trouble with the Nazi party and its leader, Adolf Hitler.

The Jews who failed to leave Germany before 1939 faced the imminent threat of internment in Nazi concentration camps. The few Weisses left in Germany, who were unable to travel due to old age, poor health, or lack of funds, along with other Jews remaining in Germany, were apprehended and transported like livestock in cramped train cars to the concentration camps.

When Germany invaded Poland on September 1st 1939, France and the United Kingdom declared war on Germany, and World War II began. In the coming months and years of the war, many Weisses still living in Europe were detained and transported to concentration camps. By the end of the war in Europe on May 9, 1945, at least six million European Jews, including many Weiss family relatives, had been apprehended, taken to concentration camps, and were either shot or killed in the gas chambers of Dachau, Buchenwald, and Sachsenhausen. The systematic murder of six million Jews was part of an over-all plan by the Nazis' called the "Final Solution" for European Jews.

* * *

Albert C. Weiss' son, Benjamin P. Weiss, was ten years old in 1940. He lived with his family in New York City, in the Borough of Manhattan, in a large home on West Broadway St. Benjamin grew up quickly in the tough Lower East Side section, which encompassed the neighborhoods between the Bowery and the East River from Canal to Houston Streets. Although Benjamin's family was affluent, when he was a young teenager, Benjamin joined a small neighborhood, predominately Jewish gang. His experience of life in a street gang, taught Benjamin how to be ruthless, cunning, and street smart. His father objected to Benjamin's involvement with the gang, but what was he to do? Some of the experiences Benjamin had in the neighborhood gang prepared him well for the corporate world in the early 1950's.

Benjamin studied business at the University of Pennsylvania, an exclusive Ivy League college. After graduating, he went to work at a well-established and successful bank owned by relatives in New York City. In 1954, he met Vanessa Goldberg, the daughter of a jewelry retailer and wholesaler. Vanessa's father owned half a dozen stores in the New York City area. In 1959, the couple had an elegant wedding ceremony in a swank Manhattan hotel ballroom. They honeymooned at the Fairmont Hotel in San Francisco, California and toured many of the Napa Valley wineries.

In 1969, Mr. and Mrs. Benjamin P. Weiss moved from a lovely, uptown Manhattan garden apartment in New York City to Grassville, Indiana, a quaint but affluent small community about one-hundred miles southwest of Indianapolis. Over the course of his career, Benjamin Weiss established a regional empire of small retail banks, all within a seventy-five-mile radius of Grassville.

Chapter 2

Benjamin and Vanessa Weiss thought they were unable to have children, but in 1970 David S. Weiss was born to the happy couple. The happiness was short lived. David's mother Vanessa died several days after childbirth.

Benjamin handpicked a live-in nanny, Miriam Gleiser, a thirty-eight-year-old, displaced German Jew, to raise and take care of his young son, David. Gleiser was an attractive woman with golden blond hair and blue eyes. When David was old enough to notice, he thought that his nanny resembled his Mother, who he only knew through photographs. Miriam was bright, energetic, and full of life. David knew his father liked her, and David liked her as well. He secretly wished that his father would marry Miriam. She was always very good to him and treated him as if he were her own child.

Miriam pampered David as a young child, but she also tried to discipline him. That was not an easy task, because Benjamin usually let his son have his own way. When David did not get what he wanted, he was hard to deal with. By the time he entered high school, David had a savings account with thousands of dollars in it and a well-funded investment account with common stocks, bonds, and mutual funds. He usually carried lots of cash in his wallet. He could buy anything he wanted and have anything he wanted. He always drove the flashiest and most expensive automobiles to school. David was accustomed to all the finer things in life. Benjamin made sure of it.

They lived just outside of Grassville in a palatial fourteen-room mansion with a large swimming pool and riding stables on a one-hundred-acre plot of hilly and beautifully landscaped land. Together, Benjamin and Vanessa had designed the property to fit their tastes before they moved from New York City to Grassville. It was Benjamin's desire to spare no expense to please his wife Vanessa.

The two-story mansion resembled the front view of the White House. The mansion had equally divided windows on each side of the front portico with pillars supporting the roof. A circular driveway in front of the house allowed convenient access for visitors and deliveries. Benjamin hired a professional design firm in Indianapolis to decorate and furnish the house. A team of landscapers maintained and manicured the lawn, bushes, and trees on the estate. The property was graced with a duck pond, white-fenced fields, and riding paths through a woods. Benjamin hired a professional groomer to tend to the horses he kept in the stables at the back of the property. He spent a lot of money to purchase five of the finest thoroughbred horses in the United States. To anyone driving by the grounds of the estate, it would be obvious that a very important and wealthy family lived there.

Benjamin Weiss' son David, a member of the graduating Class of 1988 from Grassville High School, was an outstanding athlete and student. He was intellectually gifted, possessed inordinate physical strength, and athletic ability. He had the physique and good looks of an Adonis with a strong profile and curly blond hair. All the girls in Grassville High wanted to date the handsome eighteen-year-old, who was six-feet-four-inches tall, weighed two hundred and ten-pounds, and had crystal blue eyes. Benjamin had given David everything he wanted as an adolescent to compensate for the fact that David had to grow up without a mother.

Benjamin never remarried after his wife passed away. David sometimes wondered whether his father had a mistress, but he never had the courage to ask. He realized from his own limited experience with women that having female companionship was important for the wellbeing of most normal men. David didn't doubt his father's love and affection for his mother. Years after her death, Benjamin told David that Vanessa's unforeseen and tragic death had broken his heart. From what David learned about his mother, it was evident that Vanessa had been a beautiful and very classy woman both inside and out. He imagined that it would be very hard for his father ever to consider a replacement. Still, David didn't care if his father had a mistress, girlfriend, or had remarried. He loved, admired, and respected his dad and he wanted him to be happy.

A portrait of his mother hung on the wall behind his father's desk. Whenever he visited his dad's richly appointed office, David stared at the picture. He often wished he'd had the opportunity to know her. But he would shrug his shoulders in acknowledgement of the fact that her premature death made that impossible. Not knowing her was the one thing in David's privileged life that he wouldn't be able to have, no matter how much money or wealth he possessed.

* * *

It was a late Friday evening, when David accidentally overheard a conversation between his father and their corporate attorney, Robert Levitt. The conversation grabbed David's attention. His father was ranting and raving about money that had been stolen by a valued and formerly trusted employee of the corporation. This was shocking, because, remarkably, such a betrayal had never happened before. Saul Workman, a senior branch manager at the Bedford, Indiana branch bank, had embezzled money from the bank through a fraudulent loan. Of course, Workman was the person who actually received the loan proceeds for his own use. To cover his tracks, Workman tried to write off the loan as uncollectible months later. However, a bank auditor smelled something suspicious about the transaction. When Levitt and the auditor worked their way through the company's books and records, they sniffed out Workman's scheme.

Levitt reported to Weiss that he had fired Workman that morning. Levitt said he'd told Workman in no uncertain terms that he needed to repay the money within three months or he would be prosecuted for the crime. Levitt nearly shouted, "I told Workman that if he failed to repay every cent he stole, I would personally see to it he'd be ruined, his family destroyed, and he'd go to prison for a very long time!"

After ranting about Workman's "god damned disloyalty!" Benjamin's tone changed. David perked up his ears. He heard his father quietly but firmly say to Levitt, "That's fine, but I want this handled differently. What if he tries to skip town before paying us back? I want you to go see him tomorrow morning. Collect as much of the money owed as you can and tell him to leave town. Keep track of where he goes for several months. And then, I want you to contact him one final time. You know what I mean."

"Yes, I understand," Levitt replied hesitantly. He paused a moment, then said, "I know what you want, but do you really want me to go to that extreme?" David noted that the attorney's voice was respectful of his boss' command, but he could tell that Levitt didn't want to "go to that extreme", whatever that meant.

"Just take care of the matter, counselor. I appreciate your concern, but that's how I want it handled," Weiss said with finality.

Levitt's tone was reluctant but compliant, as he responded, "I'll call our friend in Chicago."

"Good, I'm not going to allow anyone to steal from me without serious consequences. No one is going to make a fool of me either," Weiss replied angrily.

Levitt paused briefly again, took a deep breath and said, "No problem, but please note that I disagree with the extremity of your decision."

"Duly noted, counselor," Weiss said dismissively. He turned his back on Levitt and started walking down the hall toward his study. Levitt let himself out.

David wondered exactly what his father was ordering Levitt to do. It was obvious that his dad's trusted advisor still had concerns about the order. David knew that his father had not hired Levitt just to be a "yes man". Levitt was well-respected within the local Bar, so David was pretty sure his father wouldn't ignore the advice of his corporate counsel without a very good reason. So, his curiosity was piqued.

When he took a peek around the corner behind the wall down the hallway from where he was eavesdropping, David had seen the uneasiness in Levitt's face. What made the attorney so anxious about his father's instructions? David also felt uneasy about what he'd overheard. This was not the first time that David witnessed other men act deferentially toward his father. Of course, as a wealthy banker he was a man to be respected. Was his father also a man to be feared?

Robert Levitt was a graduate of the University of Chicago's nationally known law school. He was licensed to practice law in Indiana and Illinois, even though he hadn't been in a courtroom for ten years. He was forty-seven years old, divorced, brilliant, and extremely loyal to Benjamin Weiss. In fact, Weiss was his only client. Levitt was Jewish, small in stature, and physically fit. He was paid a preposterously high salary, had a fancy wardrobe, enjoyed an occasional martini, played golf every Thursday and Sunday, worked out five days each week, and was often seen socially with a beautiful woman on his arm. Whenever the company needed a litigator, Levitt retained other attorneys. Levitt's primary job was to help Weiss oversee and operate the banks. Levitt was Benjamin Weiss' right-hand man and chief advisor.

David's father had mentioned other investors in the business during conversations and phone calls David had overheard. But the only person Benjamin ever introduced to David, who seemed to be in his father's inner circle, was Robert Levitt. David realized Levitt was the point man for his father. In a way, Robert Levitt was the face of Weiss Financial, Inc. He handled all the announcements and public appearances for the corporation. David, however, assumed that his father made all the important decisions concerning the banking business and his other investments. The latest over-heard conversation between his father and Levitt bore out that assumption.

Weiss frequently left Grassville for several days at a time. He would tell David that he was going to check on branch banks and other investment properties he had accumulated. Those routine business trips just seemed to David to be part of his dad's normal schedule. When David learned that some of those trips were to Chicago, where his father had no banks or real estate holdings, he was perplexed. He didn't ask his father for an explanation. While Benjamin was generous in his expressions of affection for his only son, he rarely shared anything of substance about the business with David. When David was in middle school, he got wind of a rumor circulating in Grassville that Weiss Financial had a connection to the head of the Italian mafia in Chicago, Illinois. The syndicate in Chicago had the lurid name, "The Outfit". David did not try to discover whether the rumor was true or not. But he knew that sort of rumor would always hang on in the close-knit community of Grassville.

Not that his father ever explicitly said so, but David knew that he was not allowed to question his father about business. It bothered him that people in town talked about his father behind his back, about the alleged association with The Outfit. David vowed that, if he ever ran the family business, he would never be associated with criminals. Criminals could not be trusted! Would his father even consider doing business with people involved with organized crime? David doubted it.

That question got him to thinking about the topic of trust and trustworthiness, several days after overhearing the conversation between his dad and Mr. Levitt. David had taken an Advanced Placement course in ethics his senior year in high school. From that class, he had learned that trust had to be earned and not given out rashly or unwisely. David was skeptical by nature, so it made sense to him that people should have to prove themselves worthy before they could be trusted. David pondered the issue and even tried to write an essay on the subject for the Ethics class. But after racking his brain for a while he couldn't figure out how to devise an objective test to measure someone's trustworthiness. He concluded that such a test would be almost impossible to develop, at least for a high school senior. So, he quit thinking about the matter. Sports, cars, girls, and parties were more fun to think about anyway.

The Secret Pact

Chapter 3

At six-thirty the following morning, Saul Workman looked at his alarm clock. He groaned and slapped the alarm clock to stop the buzzing. His head ached and he felt slightly nauseated - the effects of excessive drinking during the previous day. He began hitting the bottle after being fired by his employer for embezzling money. Instead of sinking into a depression, Saul took his beautiful wife Anne out to eat at her favorite steakhouse. He was half drunk before they finished dinner. Anne was even more wasted. When they returned home, Saul hurriedly removed his clothes and got into bed. Anne was not far behind. They had a quick but satisfying and loving coupling in their king-sized bed, and then they both passed out.

Saul had decided to wine and dine Anne that night as the best way to break the news about getting fired. He sighed to himself thinking how best to let Anne in on the latest problem she would have to deal with. Saul knew he was an alcoholic, and so did Anne. Nevertheless, they had managed. But she had no idea that he had swindled $150,000 from the Bedford bank, where he had been employed for the past ten years. Of course, Anne would be upset when he broke the news to her, but how upset was the question. Saul decided he wouldn't tell her about stealing money from the bank. That might be the proverbial straw that broke the camel's back of their marriage. Saul knew Anne would be shocked at first, worried, and then extremely angry with him for losing such a good job. But would she divorce him? Divorce was something he wasn't interested in at the moment.

The first thing that broke through Saul Workman's consciousness as he fought through his morning hangover was, how was he going to repay the money he had embezzled? He really thought he was going to get away with it. Initially, he had managed to conceal his embezzlement from the newly hired Vice President in charge of loans, Peter Adkins. Saul made a mistake in his judgment of Adkins as an inexperienced banker. It turned out that Adkins was actually very thorough in his oversight duties, even though he was new to the banking business. But Saul was desperate.

Saul obtained approval of the loan from the loan committee without incident. He used a former client's name as the borrower. The purported applicant, Allen Curtis, had no idea he was being used by Saul to receive a loan he hadn't applied for. Curtis no longer owed the bank anything, because he had paid off his prior loan two years earlier. The collateral Saul listed for the construction loan was the deed for Allen Curtis' newly remodeled home. A copy of the deed was in the bank's records, because it was the collateral for the original loan. When Saul cooked up the scheme, he had no intention of permanently stealing money from the bank. He just planned to temporarily use the funds to cover his bills and repay the loan himself on a monthly basis. Saul could have taken out the loan himself, but then Anne would have found out and questioned him about the need for the loan.

When Robert Levitt walked into his office unannounced on Friday morning, Saul knew something was up. After discussing the situation, Levitt told Saul his only way out was to repay the funds via a legitimate loan from the bank with a three-month term. If Saul didn't agree, he would be prosecuted for fraud and embezzlement. Saul immediately agreed to the short-term loan and signed off on the paperwork. Before the ink was dry on his signature, Levitt ordered Saul to clean out his desk and leave the bank. He complied. It was a very embarrassing experience, but Saul was thankful the police weren't summoned to handcuff him and drag him out of the bank. Instead, Levitt escorted him out the back door of the bank. Saul's personal items were packed in a small box, which he carried to his car.

* * *

Anne was out of bed before Saul the morning after their evening of fine dining and excessive drinking. Before making breakfast, she intended to enjoy a relaxing hot shower. She bumped into Saul when she was stepping out of the shower. He was in the bathroom to relieve himself.

Anne was naked when they collided into each other in the steam-filled room. Saul could not help appreciating the view of her femininity. He gave her a loving kiss, and teasingly touched her lightly on her behind as she stepped around him. Then, he slumped back to their bed hoping to shake off the vestige of his hangover. He fell back to sleep as soon as his head hit the pillow. He didn't hear the doorbell ring a few minutes later.

* * *

At seven a.m. sharp, Robert Levitt pulled into Saul Workman's driveway. Levitt got out of his black Mercedes carrying a briefcase, approached the front door, and rang the doorbell. No one appeared, so he pushed on the button again. A minute later, the door opened and a young boy in a pair of red and black fireman pajamas stood looking at him through the glass storm door. "Is your Daddy home?" asked the middle-aged man in the dark suit.

The boy yawned and said to the early morning visitor, "He's in bed, but I'll go wake him up." The lad partially closed the front door and walked back toward his parents' bedroom.

A few minutes later, Saul Workman came to the door and was surprised to see Levitt standing outside his home so early in the morning. Saul was dressed in a robe and slippers. He said nervously, "I thought we were done. What can I do for you, Mr. Levitt?"

"Well, for starters you can invite me in. I need to talk to you for a few minutes," Levitt said in a serious tone.

"Come in, come in!" Saul nervously unlocked the storm door and opened the front door fully. He pointed to the living room couch and said, "Have a seat Mr. Levitt. Can I get you a cup of coffee?"

Levitt responded dryly, "Yes, thank you. No cream or sugar, please."

Saul looked back at his wife, who was standing in the kitchen making breakfast, and said, "Honey, please get Mr. Levitt a cup of black coffee."

As he waited for the coffee to arrive, Levitt looked around the home. He noticed the house was clean, neat, and well-furnished. In fact, it looked almost new. Levitt wanted to ask Workman what the hell he had been thinking. Why would someone with such a nice home and family steal money from the bank? Workman was well paid and had a good life from all appearances. There had to be problems he wasn't seeing. *There always are.* But, at this point it didn't really matter. Workman had made a big mistake and he would have to pay for it. Weiss was not a very forgiving man when his trust was violated.

Anne knew that Levitt was one of the top men at Weiss Financial and she wondered what he was doing in their living room on a Saturday morning. It certainly must be something important, she thought. Anne's hand shook as she poured coffee into a cup. She walked quickly into the living room and placed the coffee cup on an end table beside Levitt.

"Sorry honey, but we have something important to discuss," Saul said to his wife with a furrowed brow. "It won't take very long. Go ahead and finish making breakfast for you and Johnny."

"Okay," Anne replied in a fluttering voice. She forced a smile as she turned toward Levitt and said, "If you need more coffee, Mr. Levitt, just let me know." Anne glanced back at the two men as she retreated down the hall toward the kitchen.

Levitt smiled appreciatively and mouthed a "Thank you" at the shapely back of Workman's wife. *She's quite the looker*, thought Levitt. He pulled his eyes away as his mind returned to the business at hand. Levitt took a sip of coffee and then looked directly at Workman. "I talked to Mr. Weiss and he wants to be repaid within three business days, rather than in the form of a loan. He did not approve of the repayment arrangement I made with you."

Saul's eyes widened in surprise, and he spluttered, "But, but ... I thought we had a deal! Mr. Levitt, I wish I could do it, but I don't have that much cash and liquid assets. I'd have to sell our house and liquidate all of our assets. I, I ... just don't see..."

Levitt cut him off. "I'm sorry, but Mr. Weiss wants the money now. You'll have to work out the details for yourself. Maybe you can borrow the money from a relative or a friend. And, I'd suggest you put your home on the market immediately, since you're going to be leaving Bedford."

"Leaving Bedford! What do you mean? Mr. Weiss wants me to leave town?" Saul looked and sounded dumbstruck. "I can't just pick up and move. I have a family, you know. My son, Johnny is in school!" Saul wiped a line of sweat that had beaded on his forehead. "I have several investments I can sell. I just need a couple months to make arrangements. Surely, Weiss can give me that much time," he said plaintively.

Levitt shook his head. "No, I'm sorry. The deal we worked out does not work for him. In addition, Mr. Weiss has decided you need to leave Bedford as soon as possible. He doesn't want anything to get out within the community about your theft from the bank," Levitt raised an eye brow. "This is an embarrassment to him, as well as to you. He is quite upset, and his mercy extends no further than allowing you to remain out of jail."

As the shock wore off, Saul's spine stiffened and he replied angrily, "I'm sorry too, but we made a deal. You're his attorney, and even Mr. Weiss doesn't just get to renege on a deal you and I signed off on." Saul put his hands on his knees and looked fiercely back at Levitt. "We agreed that I could repay the debt in installments over three months! That's our deal!"

"Yes, I did make that deal with you. Unfortunately, Mr. Weiss will not accept those terms. That's why I am here this morning to convey the message. He isn't interested in giving you any more time. He wants the bank's money back by the end of the day on Wednesday, three business days from today. Mr. Weiss doesn't care what you have to do to get it. You stole his money and got caught. If you can't do it, I'll have to go to the authorities and have you arrested. I can assure you that it won't go well for you," Levitt looked down the hall where he could glimpse

Workman's attractive wife in the kitchen. "By the way, how old is your boy?" asked Levitt with a sober look on his face.

"Johnny is nine years old. Why do you ask?" Saul replied with an annoyed look on his face.

"Really, I'd hoped that he might be younger," Levitt said. "I'm sure I don't have to remind you, but if you fail to pay us back, we'll be forced to prosecute you to the fullest extent of the law. If convicted, I'd guess you'd be incarcerated for at least ten years. If you survive prison, behave yourself, and get lucky, you might be released in time to attend his graduation from high school," Levitt said coolly.

"Okay, okay, there's no need for threats, Mr. Levitt." Saul's confidence evaporated, but his mind still probed for a way out. "I'll pay the bank what I owe, but do you think Mr. Weiss might be willing to reconsider and give me the three months, if I agree to pay him a five-percent premium in addition to principal, interest, and costs?" Saul looked hopefully at Levitt.

"No, he won't accept any other offer," Levitt said definitively. "I can guarantee that. Just like I can almost guarantee that you'll take care of this matter before Thursday. He was very clear. All he wants is his $150,000 dollars back. But what happens next is up to you." Levitt picked up his cup of coffee and finished it off. He daintily patted his lips with a handkerchief he withdrew from his breast pocket. "I've got another business appointment this morning, so I need to leave. Please call me when you've made your arrangements and I'll stop by again and pick up the check."

Saul was trembling and didn't know whether he should extend his hand to try to shake Levitt's or exactly what he was supposed to do. So, he just said woodenly, "Well, thank you for trying to help, Mr. Levitt. I'm sure you understand why I had to ask about Mr. Weiss' willingness to extend more time for me to repay the loan." He wiped the sweat from his brow again, but tried to inject an optimistic tone into his voice. "I'll do my best to secure the money and pay back the bank on time."

Levitt arose from the couch. He did not extend his hand, but said in a seemingly cordial tone, "Thanks for the coffee, Saul. You have a beautiful family and I'd hate to be forced to put them through a criminal trial. No one wants to see you, convicted and go to jail. So, I'm sure you'll be able to meet Mr. Weiss' terms. I'll see myself out."

After Levitt departed, Saul drew a deep breath and sat down to think. He had a few days to raise the money. Saul realized he'd have to put his home on the market, as soon as possible. But before he did that, *maybe my rich uncle in Cleveland, Ohio would be willing to help me out. I could sign over the equity in the house to him. The equity in the house should be worth more than the debt I owe to the bank. Surely, my uncle will be willing to help out his favorite nephew, until the house sells.*

Fifteen minutes later, after he had eaten breakfast, Saul picked up the telephone and called his uncle, Maury Workman. He told his uncle that he was short on cash to pay for the construction of a new kitchen and bathroom to improve the house. "The job was completed a month ahead of schedule, so the contractor is demanding payment before I could arrange financing. Uncle Maury, can you float me a temporary loan, so I can get the contractor out of my hair?"

Of course, there was no new kitchen or bathroom. Saul lied to his uncle about why he needed the money. Saul Workman was a liar, functioning alcoholic, and an out-of-control gambler. He owed $55,000 to a loan shark. Saul feared that, if he didn't pay the loan shark, he might be a dead man, no matter what he owed Weiss. If that wasn't bad enough, Saul had an ongoing relationship with a stripper from Indianapolis. He'd been sending her up to $25,000 a year for rent, gifts, booze, and drugs to keep her happy. He also upgraded the size of Anne's engagement ring with $5,000 of the money he'd embezzled from the bank. The gift of the larger diamond had reignited their faltering sex life and made Anne feel more secure.

Saul felt safe that his uncle would not check out his story about putting in a new kitchen and bathroom. Uncle Maury was confined to a hospital bed dying of inoperable cancer. His uncle lived in an expensive nursing facility in Chagrin Falls, just outside of Cleveland, Ohio. He'd been there for the past two months. Uncle Maury was nearing the end of his life. His oncologist gave him six months to a year to live. Saul expected to inherit a small fortune when his uncle passed away. Uncle Maury's lawyer had sent him a copy of the will. So, the loan was really just an advance on his inheritance.

But Maury was at first hesitant to make the loan. He demanded that Saul fully explain the details of the arrangement he was asking for. Uncle Maury was eighty-six years old, but still had a relatively sharp mind. He had been a very successful businessman. He asked his nephew how much he needed and how he planned to pay it back. Saul told him the loan would be for $100,000. Saul still had close to $60,000 left from what he had stolen from Weiss Financial. The money was tucked away in his closet safe. He had used up the rest of the embezzled proceeds repaying his gambling debts, sending money to his stripper-girlfriend, and purchasing a different wedding ring for his wife. So, $100,000 was slightly more than he would need to pay back the bank. With $160,000 in cash, Saul would still have about $15,000 for a slush fund to maintain his family. He could repay Uncle Maury when the house sold, if Maury was still alive.

After hearing Saul's explanation of the need for the loan and Saul's plan to pay it back within three months, Maury assured Saul that he would wire $100,000 on Monday morning directly into Saul's bank account. Saul breathed a sigh of relief after hanging up the phone. *Thank God for Uncle Maury!* The next challenge was going to be what to tell Anne. Their lives were going to change dramatically and Anne didn't like change. Saul immediately set his devious mind to working on a strategy to put a positive spin on why they had to sell the house and move.

On Monday morning, he called Levitt and told him that he would be able to pay off the debt in full on Wednesday morning. He assured him that he would keep silent about stealing from the bank. He would not even tell his wife. They would put the house on the market and move out of town as soon as possible. Saul had already called a real estate agent and learned the property was worth about $65,000 more than what he expected. *Great!* He could use the balance on the sale of the house to make a down payment on a new home. Saul told Levitt that he and Anne were undecided where to move as of yet, but they would be out of town sooner rather than later.

Levitt thanked Workman and said he would stop by and pick up the check Wednesday afternoon. He told Workman that he was sorry how things had worked out and wished him well. Levitt remarked to Workman that he and Mr. Weiss were pleased with how well he was handling the unfortunate predicament.

Chapter 4

David Weiss began dating Angelina Mangano when they were sophomores in high school. She was the hottest girl in David's class. Many other guys in Grassville High asked Angelina out. She did go out with a few other boys, until she and David traded rings senior year. So, that left all the other Grassville teenage-boys in the unenviable position to do nothing but fantasize about what they would do with Angelina, if given the chance. The other guys she had dated prior to senior year would have done anything to be with her again, but she was now David Weiss' girlfriend. No one at school had the guts to cross David Weiss. Everybody had heard the rumors about his father. And David was not someone you wanted to mess with either. He was physically imposing and never backed down when challenged. David was known to have a hot temper and was not afraid to kick the ass of any kid who messed with him.

Angelina was a dark-haired brunette, who stood five-foot four-inches tall and had the curves that would accelerate any heterosexual guy's hormones into overdrive. She was also exceedingly smart, the captain of the cheer leaders, and President of the Senior Class. Angelina's soft white skin and brown eyes perfectly set off her shapely figure. As if that wasn't enough, she also had an engaging personality. She was passionate about the ideals she believed in, and she had a kind and loving nature.

David knew he had a winner in Angelina. The one thing about her that didn't quite make sense to David was her need to be so close to her family. Angelina came from a very wealthy Italian family. Her father owned a manufacturing plant in southern Indiana, which supplied automobile parts for General Motors. The two kids seemed a perfect match. The whole town assumed that David and Angelina would get married, sooner rather than later. They both planned to enter Indiana University in Bloomington in the fall. David was expected to major in finance and play football for the Hoosiers. Angelina wanted to study psychology.

In David's mind it all seemed to be working out perfectly. Still, as an only child of a single parent, he felt uncomfortable about the control Angelina's father seemed to have over her. He wondered why she so often wanted to hang out at her own house, especially when her parents and brothers and sisters were around. He loved his own father, but had lived such an independent life without much of a family. The way the Manganos stuck together was something David had a hard time wrapping his mind around.

Howard White was David's closest and best friend. He was extremely bright, friendly, and unlike David, was not Jewish but a member of the Episcopal Church. He was an athlete but not as talented as David. Howard was smaller than David at six-feet tall and weighed one-hundred fifty pounds. He had dark black hair and was ranked number two on the cross-country team. Howard enjoyed swimming in the Weiss' large in-ground pool and riding their thorough bred horses. The two boys were inseparable. Whenever you saw David there was Howard, and vice-a-versa. Howard's grandfather was an industrialist, who passed on a small fortune to Howard's father. Howard was a brilliant student and was offered several academic scholarships at Ivy League schools. He wanted to pursue a political science degree and then attend law school. David was sure Howard would succeed at whatever he set his mind to. He thought his friend could become a great attorney. He laughingly, but seriously, told Howard he should be a lawyer, because he was so devious and cunning. Howard could not beat David in any games that required strength and speed, but he routinely bested his buddy in games, like chess, that required strategic thinking.

Steven Mills was another close friend of both David and Howard. He was very tall, thin, tanned, and full of life. Steven had brown hair and eyes, and was a natural athlete even though he had no interest or time to play sports. His Dad owned several large hardware stores in Grassville, Bloomington, and Vincennes, Indiana. He worked for his father in the Grassville store as he was growing up. Steven's scholastic ability was not as impressive as either David's or Howard's, but he was a very likeable guy and loyal friend to both of them. He had plans to attend Ball State University to earn a business degree. In addition to business, Steven was interested in history, political science, and politics. He had ambitions to run for state representative in the Indiana legislature. His family was not wealthy, but they were very comfortable.

David sometimes wondered whether Steven was envious of his and Howard's wealth and the superior social status of their families. The three friends occasionally talked about their own hopes and dreams beyond high school. Steven made it clear that he not only wanted a political career, but he also wanted to become wealthy, like his two friends were.

Howard and Steven both had girlfriends that were smart, attractive, and talented. Howard's girlfriend was Staci Lykaios. She was of Greek descent. Her parents owned and operated two popular restaurants, one in Grassville and the other in Bedford, Indiana. After going out for over a year, Staci and Howard thought they had a future together. She was short at five-foot one-inch tall with olive-colored skin and jet-black hair. Her large, medium-brown eyes intrigued him. Staci planned to attend college even though her parents wanted her to begin preparing to take over the restaurants, when they were ready to retire.

Ann Gottlieb was tall and blond with a perfect lily-white complexion. She was not strikingly beautiful like the other two women, but Steven Mills was captivated by her looks, blue eyes, delightful personality, and wit. Ann was accepted at the University of Notre Dame. She intended to major in elementary education. She was especially interested in working with at-risk children. Ann was idealistic, but thought pragmatically that she would be able to be a positive influence in the lives of troubled kids and to help them succeed in life. Gottlieb's parents were divorced and her German-immigrant father was a medical research doctor, who worked in a laboratory in Indianapolis. Like Steven, Ann was not rich, but she had a very comfortable upbringing, despite her parents' divorce.

David knew he and his friends had different life goals and agendas, and they might never be as close as they had been in high school. But he thought they were all on trajectories that would likely lead each of them to unique accomplishments and achievements in the future. His career path was all but decided. Someday, he would manage the Weiss Investment Group. David looked forward to realizing his own future, and was undaunted imagining himself taking over the business from his father. He tried to appear to be as humble as possible around his friends and classmates, although he knew that they knew his privileges and opportunities far exceeded what other kids in Grassville had to look forward to after graduation.

David sometimes wondered whether or not his friends were honest to goodness true friends or not. As the sole heir to the vast fortune that his father had accumulated, David knew other kids might want to hang out with him, because, who knows, maybe he could give them a job someday. He was sure Howard and Steven were as loyal to him as he was to them. At least, he thought they were. But going back to the question of trust, did he really know how far he could trust even his best two buddies? The question was perplexing.

Occasionally, he pondered whether or not his friends had any hidden agendas. He knew he did, so he presumed they did as well. David Weiss was confident, conflicted, paranoid, complex, and narcissistic. He actually had little or no interest in the agendas of others, only his own. While he usually said all the right things to appear to be a concerned friend, when Howard and Steven, or other guys they hung out with, talked about the future, David really didn't give a damn about anyone's future, except his own. Once in a while, his public persona slipped to reveal a spoiled brat. And why wouldn't he be, given his upbringing, wealth, and precocious status in life. Nevertheless, he normally behaved properly, was friendly to others, and actually generous to others in his social circle. David wondered whether any of his friends saw through his veneer. If they did, not even Howard or Steven said so. He wished he could be accepted as he was with his flaws, imperfections, and weaknesses. But he had decided at a young age that it was safer to always try to appear to be flawless. In fact, he had played the role so long, it had become difficult even to ever admit to himself that he wasn't perfect.

Chapter 5

Joel Dalton was a smelly, ill-bred hillbilly and unpopular member of the Grassville High School junior class. His usual attire consisted of a perspiration stained, red and white Indiana University ball cap, a NASCAR T-shirt, a pair of worn jeans, and tattered sneakers.

Joel and his alcoholic, drug-addicted father, Lowell Dalton, lived in a small, two-bedroom rundown shack on a dirt road just outside of the city limits of Grassville. The house was on a dead-end street. It stunk of cigarette smoke, old grease, and mildew. The furniture was shabby and food stained. Uneven and stained wall-paper was the highlight of the house's interior décor. Wood rot and peeling paint adorned the exterior walls. The "landscaping" consisted of clumps of tall grass in an unkempt yard.

Joel was almost six-feet tall and weighed 140 pounds soaking wet. He had dirty, stringy, long brown hair and wore clothing purchased at the local Goodwill store. Several of his teeth were missing, because his father knocked them out during a drunken stupor. Joel's teeth weren't replaced, because he had not seen a doctor or dentist for years. His remaining teeth were stained a yellowish-brown. There were usually unhealed scabs on his elbows and knees and pimples on his face. His breath had an unhealthy odor. Not surprisingly, Joel's classmates at Grassville High avoided him as much as possible. He had the reputation of being a thief, and none of the other kids trusted him.

Joel considered himself half-Jewish, because his mother was Jewish. He had never been inside a synagogue, never read the Bible, and knew nothing about the Jewish faith. But he liked the idea of being Jewish, because it gave him some sense of an identity different from most of his Hoosier neighbors and classmates. Joel didn't particularly believe in God. What had God ever done for him? He didn't consider himself to be an atheist so much as he just didn't give a damn about a god who didn't give a damn about him.

Several years after marrying Lowell Dalton, Joel's mother Sarah, abandoned her husband and son. Joel was three years old when she left. Sarah told anyone who would listen that she left because Lowell didn't make enough money to support them. So that was the explanation Lowell gave, when little Joel started asking what happened to his momma. When he was old enough to think more clearly about what had happened to his mother, he doubted the veracity of the story. When Joel was thirteen, one of his aunts told him that Sarah ran away with a younger man who had been her lover for years.

Lowell Dalton was a wife beater and a cheat. He was going out with other women the entire time he was married to Sarah. So, their infidelity was mutual. Neither of Joel's parents took much interest in him. A couple of his aunts tried to look after Joel, and he was in and out of the custody of the Lawrence County Child Protective Services. Temporary placements were made with relatives and foster parents, but eventually he ended up back in the crappy old house with his dad. Despite his father's abuse and inattentiveness as a parent, Joel managed to stay in school. Dedicated teachers, the aunts, and foster parents provided enough of a basis for support that he was able to advance with his class toward high school graduation.

Lowell Dalton was incarcerated several times for minor crimes as a youth. When he was nineteen, he was convicted of manslaughter and theft. He did an eight-year stint at the Indiana State Prison in Michigan City for those crimes. Lowell was a two-hundred eighty-pound, six-foot two-inch bully. He wasn't scared of anybody or anything. Inmates at the penitentiary were afraid of him, not only because of his size and temper. They thought he was crazy. Lowell grew up on the south side of Chicago. He learned to fight on those mean streets, and he learned that, if you were in a fight, always throw the first punch. Drunk or sober, Lowell's favorite saying was, "I have little to lose and nothing to live for, so that's why I ain't afraid of nothing and nobody." When Joel was a child, and he would hear his father muttering that axiom, it made him feel terrible. *What about me,* he thought, *I'm your son. Aren't I worth living for*? By the time Joel was a teenager, he'd concluded that he was worthless in his father's eyes.

When Lowell was drunk, Joel was a favorite target. When Lowell was sober, if Joel screwed something up, he took a beating from his father. Sometimes neighbors made anonymous telephone calls to the Grassville police when they heard Joel screaming. The police came when called, but they usually didn't bother making an arrest. The cops would calm Lowell down and make sure Joel wasn't hurt too badly. If they took Lowell in, Joel would go back into the rotating door of Child Protective Services. After another temporary placement Joel would be back in his father's custody, and the cycle would start over again. Small town cops figured it was just more efficient to maintain the status quo, until Lowell crossed the line and left too many obvious cuts or bruises on Joel's face. Plus, Joel was too afraid to rat on his father, so he always denied any abuse had taken place.

Joel dreamed of leaving Grassville and Lowell for good, but he had no idea how he could pull that off. He didn't know where he'd go, if he left. He didn't know where his mother was. No one else in the family had the means to support him and he didn't even have enough money for one night in a cheap motel.

Joel was expected to clean up any mess his father made, and to wash their clothes and the dirty dishes on a daily basis. By the time he was in junior high school, Lowell demanded that Joel earn money to help pay for his father's cigarettes, booze, and drugs. Since no employer was willing to offer Joel a job, he had to turn to theft to avoid more beatings by Lowell. Not that Joel really wanted to get a regular job anyway. It was easier to steal than to work for a paycheck. Joel quickly realized he could make money quicker and easier by stealing. His father approved.

When Joel was a novice, inexperienced thief, he was afraid he might get caught. But he was more concerned about what his father would do to him, if he didn't bring home sufficient cash. And, as long as he was doing what his dad wanted, even if he were apprehended by the authorities, he knew he could rely on Lowell to bail him out of jail. One fatherly interest Lowell took in his son was to teach him how to become a career thief. However, given Joel's intellectual limitations, early into his career he was caught on two occasions. Joel was placed in a juvenile detention center for six months. When he was released, Lowell gave him fatherly advice about being more cautious during a robbery. Next, Lowell gave his son an advanced course in burglary. Lowell taught Joel how to pre-select his targets.

"Son, you have to find the most vulnerable homes in the nicer neighborhoods. Those are the plum targets." Lowell explained that you had to be patient and wait until you were sure the occupants of the homes were gone before breaking in. Entering through the back door or an open window on the backside of a house was always preferable than trying to break in on the street-facing side. "Look for the cover of trees, bushes, anything to block the view of neighboring homes and anybody out on the street or sidewalk, when you make your move. And you gotta check for alarm systems. If you can't disable it, leave that house alone and find another one. When you're inside, find the stereos, computers, jewelry, collectibles, and cash. Then get the hell out."

Lowell had a girlfriend and he spent as many nights at her place as at home. That left Joel to fend for himself, which was alright with Joel. He felt safer when his father wasn't home. Joel was very conflicted in his feelings for his father. He loathed him and fantasized about beating the shit out of his dad. On the other hand, Lowell was about the only constant in Joel's life, and, like it or not, Lowell was his father. Joel once asked the richest kid in town to help him get away from Lowell. But the kid refused his request. Joel pleaded his case, but apparently not well enough to change the other kid's mind. After that, Joel figured he was stuck with his dad, until something happened. What that could be, he wasn't sure. Maybe his dad would get so drunk, he'd run his car off a bridge or get shot in a bar. Whatever.

During Joel's junior year in high school, something did happen. He met a more experienced crook from Bedford, Indiana. Tommy Cochrane was the leader of a small gang that specialized in stealing and reselling new and used farm implements. They fenced the stolen goods in northeastern Indiana. Cochrane was looking to add another person to his gang, when he heard about this kid who was developing a reputation as a competent burglar and thief. Cochrane offered to give Joel a tryout for entry into his gang. His first job would be to act as a lookout during the robberies. But Cochrane promised Joel that, if he proved himself worthy, Joel would be trained for other positions within the gang in due time. He also told Joel that his future with the gang would depend on his performance, attitude, loyalty, and guts.

Cochrane had heard about Joel from a corrupt pawn shop owner in Bedford. The pawnbroker told Cochrane that Joel dependably brought in decent merchandise. When

Cochrane made the offer to Joel, he said, if the gang accepted him, Joel would learn how to handle higher end burglaries and he'd make more money with the gang than doing jobs on his own. At first, Joel was thrilled just to be noticed. Wow! Maybe this was his way out from under his father's thumb. *Maybe, I could get enough money to leave home and get a fresh start.* But then he hesitated. He didn't know what it would be like to be in a gang and have to get along with a bunch of other guys and take orders from somebody other than his dad. Maybe he should turn down the offer. Cochrane was an ex-con and professional thief. Would it really be any better working for him than for Lowell? *What if something went wrong and I got arrested again?* Even more worrisome, what would his father do when he found out? But Cochrane was clearly not a man to get on the wrong side of. So, Joel decided to take what he thought would be the safest way out of his dilemma. He agreed to work with Cochrane without telling his father. He would keep the funds he earned with Cochrane for himself, but he would also keep doing his own jobs to keep Lowell off his back.

There were times when Joel wondered whether he could survive another beating by his father. Joel had become very tough for his age and skinny physique. He guessed that was one benefit from the physical abuse he'd endured. Still, he dreamed about leaving his dad and this crappy shack they shared. But what would he do with his life, if all of a sudden, he became free and independent? Truck driving appealed to him. It would be cool to travel and see the country. He'd never even been outside southern Indiana, but he could picture himself behind the wheel of a big rig driving through the Rocky Mountains and out to California. He'd always heard that truckers had steady work and a pretty good paycheck just for driving. Joel wasn't exactly sure what the requirements were to become a commercial driver, but it couldn't be too hard to learn how to drive a semi and pull a trailer, could it?

When Joel dreamed about driving a big rig across the country, he also dreamed about having a girlfriend. They'd listen to the Rolling Stones driving during the day and have sex in a bed in the back of the cab every night. The image of driving with his girlfriend and listening to their favorite tunes always made him smile. When he got to the sex part of the dream, he'd feel a bulge growing in his crotch.

In reality, Joel never had a girlfriend, though, he desperately wanted one. One time, he went out with Sheila Riley, a young, under-aged, neighborhood girl, and got her drunk. While she was drunk, they had sex. Joel was not wearing any protection and the girl was not on the pill. Unfortunately, the girl's mother caught them in the back seat of her Chevy Impala, parked inside the garage. Joel received an intense ass-chewing from the girl's mother, who threatened to call the police and have him arrested for rape. Then, Dan Riley, Sheila's Dad, came into the house and learned what his daughter had been doing with Joel. Riley was actually a reasonable guy, who understood that young people did stupid things like this. He explained to Joel that, if Sheila got pregnant, Joel would be responsible to pay for her hospital bills as well as for the baby's on-going care and support over the next eighteen years. Then, Mr. Riley told Joel to get the hell out of his house and never see Sheila again. Of course, he would have liked to give Joel a good thrashing, but the thought of repercussions from Lowell Dalton deterred him. Who knew what that criminally dangerous and unpredictable ex-con might do, if he learned Riley had whipped his boy. Riley judiciously kept his temper under control and did not lay a hand on Lowell's pip squeak of a son.

As his junior year wound down, it dawned on Joel that the annual school prom was coming up. It was held every year in the Grassville High School gymnasium. The idea popped into his mind that the dance would afford an opportunity to steal stuff, like booze, drugs, and cash from the cars of the juniors and seniors, while they were inside the gym during the prom. Joel knew Prom Night was a big deal to the in-crowd kids and a couple hundred cars would be in the parking lot during the dance and other festivities.

He could hardly wait for the weekend to arrive. One of his dad's lessons in breaking and entering, covered automobiles. Joel was sure that the chumps who went to the prom would leave plenty of valuable stuff in their vehicles during the dance. He considered enlisting his buddy, Harvey Benson, to help. Harvey owned a car and was one of the few other kids willing to hang out with Joel. But after further consideration, Joel decided to cut Harvey out of the job. If I can make enough money from this job, it could be my chance to get the hell away from my dad. I might even make enough money to leave this shit hole of a town behind. Hmm, but I need a driver for a get-away car. I'll bet that whore of a girlfriend of my dad's would do it for a little taste of the loot. She's a cagey bitch and smart enough to keep her mouth shut for a little dough.

Joel planned to be very selective about who he stole from. The most expensive stuff would probably be in the richest kid's cars. Joel smiled to himself thinking about which of the dozen or so of the richest kid's vehicles he'd break into. This was his chance to get over on those preppies before they graduated.

Chapter 6

The entire town of Grassville was looking forward to the high school graduation ceremonies, which were to be held in the recently rehabbed Virgil (Gus) Grissom Memorial auditorium on Saturday, June 4th, 1988. The high school campus, along with the auditorium, had been upgraded and remodeled during the Class of 1988's four years at GHS. Classrooms were modernized with the additions of new desks, chairs, and audio-visual equipment. Wooden window frames in the main building were replaced with new and improved vinyl coated frames. Word processors were installed in the administrative office. Calculators were provided for all math and science classes, and the online encyclopedia Nexus was made available through a new computer installed in the school library.

The costs of improvement to the physical plant and new equipment and technology for the high school were covered by a fifteen-year bond issued by the school corporation. The bank which handled the issuance of the bond was owned by the most prominent man in the county, Benjamin Weiss. Weiss maintained a high profile in the communities his banks served. Although it was rumored that Weiss had connections with notorious figures in the Chicago underworld, he actively supported many charitable causes and organizations in the Grassville area. For instance, in 1987 Weiss donated the land for a new community park in Grassville. Most members of the community thought it was a blessing to have him as a local resident regardless of the rumors about his connection to the mob. In fact, Benjamin Weiss was respected as a banker, entrepreneur, and philanthropist throughout southern Indiana.

Grassville is located about one-hundred miles southwest from Indianapolis. The population was just under ten thousand in the 1980 census. Local businesses lined Main Street. Only a few chain stores and fast food restaurants had penetrated the retail market of Grassville by 1988. The big box stores had not yet arrived in town, but the Chamber of Commerce feared Walmart was on the horizon. Grassville was the county seat of Lawrence County. Most of the area's professional class lived in Grassville. Outside the city limits of Grassville were a few small, unincorporated communities as well as wide expanses of farmland, several small streams, dense hardwood and pine forests, hilly terrain, and narrow winding roadways.

The town of Grassville had the distinction of being designated an All-American City by the National Civic League. Brick streets were preserved in the downtown historical-district. The majority of homes in Grassville were well kept with freshly painted exteriors and well-tended lawns. The town exuded the Midwestern values of pride in home ownership and responsibility to your community. Its commercial and industrial base was thriving. There was a central park with a community swimming pool and several neighborhood parks with ball fields. Visitors to Grassville are greeted with signs reading, "Welcome to Grassville, an All-American City, Michael Brown, Mayor."

* * *

Most of the folks in the Grassville area were Indiana University and Robert Montgomery Knight basketball fans. When the Indiana Hoosiers won their fifth NCAA Championship and the third under Coach Knight in 1987, David's father was court-side, sitting right next to the team in Assembly Hall. When Benjamin Weiss wasn't traveling, he would frequently take David to Indiana University basketball and football games. Benjamin served on the prestigious endowment committee for IU. He hoped David would attend Indiana University in Bloomington.

During David's junior year in high school, Benjamin arranged a meeting for David with Coach Bill Mallory. Mallory was the head football coach of the Indiana Hoosiers. He told David that, if he came to IU, he would have an excellent chance of becoming the starting quarterback his freshman year. Mallory was so impressed with David that he invited David back to Bloomington early in David's senior year in high school to visit the campus. David attended the season opener against Rice University, met with some of the returning players for the following season, and toured the football facilities. Mallory genuinely liked David. He recognized his natural leadership qualities, admired his work ethic, and appreciated David's sterling academic record. With those qualities and David's outstanding athletic ability, Coach Mallory thought he would make an excellent quarterback for the Indiana football program. So, after reviewing David's high school career, watching his workouts, accessing his play, and watching tapes of David's high school games, Mallory offered David a full-ride athletic scholarship.

David was thrilled when he received the offer. His dream was coming true. He would play football for the IU Hoosiers, study business in IU's renowned Kelley School of Business, and still get to be with Angelina, who was already accepted in the Social Science program to study psychology. David happily accepted Coach Mallory's offer.

* * *

The Grassville High School graduating Class of 1988 consisted of 160 students. Following the graduation and commencement ceremonies in the school's auditorium, per local tradition the graduating seniors and their dates were invited to a steak dinner hosted by the Grassville business community. After conclusion of the dinner, all the kids convened in the school's gymnasium. Also, by tradition, the Senior Celebration doubled as Grassville High's version of the junior/senior prom. The school gym was decked out with festive decorations and mementoes of the graduates' high school experiences. The high point of the celebrations from the students' point of view was a DJ dance party. The only adults at the dance were the teachers who were the senior class sponsors. The male graduates wore tuxedos and the girls wore formal prom dresses. Some of the more affluent kids had their parents rent stretch limos and came to the celebration in groups of six or eight. Others came with their dates in dad's Cadillac or sports car. The less affluent graduates drove up in their pick-up trucks and older sedans.

With the traditions of commencement and the formal dinner in the rear view mirror the graduates and their dates finally let loose in the gym to shake their booties during the fast dances and then to snuggle up close during the slow dances. The DJ played tunes of the popular recording artists of the 1980's, like The Cars, REO Speedwagon, Whitesnake, ZZ Top, and Guns N' Roses, Madonna, Cindi Lauper, Michael Jackson, Willie Nelson, and Garth Brooks. The DJ played music on cassette players and turntables, utilizing mixers and a variety of expensive stereo speaker systems specifically designed for large rooms, big crowds, and gala events. Most of the graduates partied and danced the night away, until the music stopped and the lights were turned out.

During the dance, kids slipped out to drink Natural, Bud, or Miller Lite beer stashed in coolers in cars in the parking lot. Seagram's wine coolers, cheap tequila, Kentucky bourbon, and shots of whiskey, along with cigarettes and marijuana joints, were passed around from car to car. Inside the glove boxes the graduates stored their wallets, purses, and Trojans. The senior guys were counting on the alcohol and pot to prime their dates for a successful sendoff following their graduation. The plan of many of the graduates was to go out after the dance ended to park in their girlfriend's driveways or at a secluded spot on a dirt road out in the country popularly known as "lover's lane". The expectation was there would be a lot of kissing, petting, and then, hopefully, the Trojan would be put to use. Many of the girls, who were still virgins, decided they too were ready to go all the way that evening. For some of the couples, graduating signaled that it was time for them to experience sex. While "going all the way" in the back seat of a parent's, friend's or boyfriend's car or truck, does not seem very romantic to a sophisticated adult, to seventeen and eighteen-year old's in a small town in Indiana in 1988 it was the perfect setting.

Unobserved by the celebrating seniors and their dates, Joel Dalton, lurked around the perimeter of the gymnasium parking lot. Joel wasn't there for the dinner, dance, or even to hang out and drink beer and smoke pot. Instead, he was scoping out the more expensive vehicles to steal cash, alcohol, drugs, condoms, or whatever valuables he could find. Dalton was wearing dark clothing. He carried a pair of pliers, a straightened clothes hanger, a flash light, a small screwdriver, and a black bag. His father had tutored him in how to unlock an automobile and pop its trunk. Dalton had spent the evening breaking into cars, opening trunks, and choosing what was worth stealing.

Dalton was careful to watch for partiers sneaking out of the gym to have a drink, smoke a cigarette or a joint, make out, or cop a feel of their girlfriend's breasts. He slunk into a shadow or knelt behind one of the vehicles whenever someone might be looking in his direction. Dalton had accumulated quite a collection of booze, pot, and valuables, so that his black bag was beginning to bulge with treasure. He was almost ready to leave, but there was one more car he specifically wanted to find before he called it a night.

Joel Dalton had never forgiven David Weiss for blowing him off in his time of need. He was determined to get a little payback before that rich SOB went off to college. There it was, the 1988 Audi with the IU Hoosiers custom plate. Joel recognized the car he'd seen David driving around town in. He was sure there would be plenty of good stuff to steal in Weiss' car.

But just as he started to jimmy the trunk open, Dalton heard voices approaching. David Weiss was walking toward the car with a group of his friends. Dalton immediately dropped to his knees and crawled under Weiss' Audi to hide. But "Shit!" he hissed to himself. In his haste he dropped the flashlight. It rolled under the rear bumper of the car. Nothing he could do about that now. Joel lay prostrate under the car carefully controlling his breathing so as not to be discovered. He waited patiently for the group to leave.

There were six kids standing around Weiss' car, David, his girlfriend, Angelina Mangano, and David's two best buddies, Howard White and Steven Mills, and their girlfriends, Staci Lykaios and Ann Gottlieb. Dalton knew that, if he got caught, the three boys would easily overpower him and beat him up. He quickly looked at his Timex to check the time. He noted it was eleven-fifteen p.m. Sally agreed to be in the parking lot just after eleven. Joel hoped to God she would be there on time.

Weiss popped open the trunk of his expensively hand-crafted, red 1988 Audi 5000. He handed cold beers to each member of the group and mixed a rum and coke for himself. This was the fourth time during the dance the group had paid a visit to David's mobile bar, as he laughingly called it. Everyone in the group was either tipsy or drunk. David was definitely drunk on rum and coke. While Weiss was leaning against the back of the car and shakily serving out drinks, he stepped on something round. *Hmm*, wonder what that is, he thought. Making sure not to lose his balance, he carefully bent down and picked it up. That was odd, why was a flashlight under the rear bumper of his car? And, why hadn't he noticed it during the group's previous trips to his mobile bar?

David pushed the switch and the light came on. Suspicion broke through the alcohol vapors in his brain. *Something wasn't right!* With the flashlight on he took hold of the bumper with his left hand and leaned down to shine the light under the car. To David's surprise, there was a body stretched out on the ground under his Audi.

When the light was cast on him, Joel realized he was in trouble. As quickly as he could, he scooted up to the front of the car away from the six pairs of feet behind the car. But it took a few agonizing seconds to claw his way out from under the car on the asphalt surface and then get to his feet. Shit! The bag of loot caught on the car's bumper.

Have to leave it. Joel began running as fast as he could. Have to make it to my get-away car before I get caught! God, Sally better be there!

When David saw the body under his car, he yelled out, "Hey! What the hell!" As Joel began scrambling out from under the car, David shook his head to clear it of drunken dizziness and started running after the figure fleeing across the parking lot. Howard and Steven immediately followed.

Joel was wispy thin and quick, but his speed was no match for three of the best athletes in Grassville High School. David caught up with the darkly-clad figure and clothes-lined him with a powerful forearm across the back of the neck. The kid tumbled to the ground. David was standing over him breathing hard with clenched fists when his two friends caught up. Howard and Steven grabbed Joel by his upper arms and picked him up. When they recognized Dalton, they shook their heads and muttered that it was no surprise such a scumbag was caught messing around with someone else's car. David aimed the bright light of Dalton's own flashlight into his beady dark eyes and demanded angrily, "What were you doing under my car?"

Joel rubbed some blood off of his chin, which got scraped when David knocked him to the ground. He looked around at the faces staring at him. He knew he was going to have a hard time talking his way out of this predicament, but he had to try. He looked down at the ground and said, "I, uh, just dropped my flashlight and I was looking for it."

"Then, why did you hide under my car and run away

from me?"

"I was afraid you might think I was trying to do something to your car, but I wasn't," Dalton said nervously. "I was just looking for my flashlight, that's all."

Just then, Angelina, Staci, and Ann came walking up to the guys. Angelina called out, "Look what I found!" She held up a heavy black bag. She explained that she'd found it under the front bumper of David's car. She turned the bag over and dumped out its contents. Purses, wallets, drugs, condoms, and several bottles of Whiskey tumbled out. One of the last items to drop out of the bag was a small sequined pursue. Staci's eyes widened and she grabbed the purse off the pile of stolen items. She opened the purse and held up her school ID and driver's license for the others to see. Howard let out a bellow, "You son of a bitch! Staci put her purse in the glove box of my car!" He looked around at the other kids and said, "This prick broke into my car."

David demanded furiously, "Where did you get Staci's purse and the rest of this stuff?"

Joel's voice took on a pleading tone, "The bag doesn't belong to me. I found it on the ground over by the chain link fence next to the big tree," he said pointing back in the direction of a large oak tree beside the school parking lot. "I was going to call the police and turn that stuff in at the police station," Dalton said looking around wide-eyed and desperate.

"You fucking lying, little thief!" Weiss shouted at Dalton. "I'm going to teach you a God damn lesson you'll never forget!" Howard and Steven grabbed Dalton's arms and held on to him tightly. Weiss hit him squarely on the chin. The force of the punch was so powerful it knocked Dalton out of the grasp of the other two boys. Joel landed flat on his back. Still enraged, Howard and Steven pulled Joel up and Weiss slugged him again, this time directly on the nose. Blood spewed out of Dalton's nose. The boys let Joel's limp body drop to the ground. Howard and Steven began kicking him in the stomach, ribs, and chest. They were breathing hard when they stopped. But David wasn't finished with Joel. He stepped up and kicked Joel under the chin snapping his head back. As David was about to deliver another kick to the limp body, Howard White stepped in and pulled David away. It was evident that Dalton was badly hurt and needed medical attention. Still, Weiss looked down at Joel, pointed his finger at him, and said loudly, "Asshole, if I ever catch you doing this again, I'll kill you."

Dalton didn't move. When the boys first started kicking him, Joel had covered his head and curled up into the fetal position to try to protect himself. But after David's last kick, Joel's body went lax and he didn't move.

Howard White bent down and tried to help Dalton up. It felt like he was lifting a dead weight. A tremor of fear shot down Howard's spine. He looked up at David and said, "I think he's unconscious or dead."

"Oh shit," David muttered. "Howard, check his pulse. Is he still breathing?"

White felt for a pulse on Joel's wrist. "I, I don't feel one." Then a wave of nausea swept up from Howard's stomach, which was full of beer mixed with a couple shots of whiskey. He almost wretched and felt too lightheaded to check for further signs of life. Howard struggled to his feet and leaned against David.

"Oh, my God, what do we do now?" David said in desperation. Beads of sweat started dripping down his forehead and his hands began shaking. "Is there anybody else around? Did anyone see us in the parking lot?" David asked nervously as he quickly gazed around the parking lot.

"I don't see anyone. I think ours was the only group out in the parking lot, when we caught the bastard," White said. He'd regained his composure and his voice took on a cold, calculating tone. "But we need to act quickly before someone comes outside and sees what happened."

"What should we do with Dalton?" Weiss asked, gripping Howard's shoulder.

"We can move his body to a different location," White replied coolly.

"Are you serious?" Angelina said as she grabbed hold of David's trembling hand. She turned and looked into the eyes of each of the three boys. Steven looked shocked and edged away from Dalton's body. Ann was shaking like a leaf, but Staci spit on the prostrate body of Joel Dalton.

Howard ignored Angelina and calmly proposed, "David, let's load him in the trunk of your car and we'll drop him in the Whitcomb Woods several miles east of town. He's a nobody. He won't be missed and his body will never be found. What do you say?" White looked up at Weiss waiting for his friend's response.

David shook his head and pulled away from Angelina. "Jesus Christ," he muttered. But after just a moment of delay, he agreed. "Okay, let's do it." David's typical determination kicked in. "Angelina, you, Staci and Ann need to leave right now. Steven, drive the girls home. Okay?

"Sure, uh, I can do that, David, no problem," Steven said breathlessly. He no longer felt drunk. In fact, Steven Mills was cold sober. He was scared and nervous and he wanted to get the hell out of there as quickly as possible.

"Howard, you and I will take care of Dalton, but first, we all have to agree never to talk about this hillbilly bastard and what happened ever again. Not to anyone, okay? Angelina, Steven, Staci, and Ann, I'm counting on you to be cool. We won't get into trouble over this situation if we all stick together and keep our mouths shut. Do you understand?" David instinctively knew he could count on Howard White, so he turned and stared first at Steven and then at each of the girls, probing them with his eyes for any sign of dissent or weakness.

Angelina spoke first, "Yes, I understand, David."

Steven nodded, "Yeah, me too. Never say anything about it to anybody," he said woodenly looking away from the others.

Staci gave a thumbs up. Ann was still shaking, but she nodded affirmatively.

"Okay, then," David said feeling somewhat relieved. "If you see anyone back in the parking lot that asks what we were doing, just tell them that we chased off a thief. People are going to realize somebody broke into a bunch of cars tonight. But we don't know who it was, and we've just been out here enjoying a last round of drinks and a final toke. Don't act like anything is wrong. Angelina, just leave Dalton's bag minus Staci's purse where you found it, under the tree. But first, check inside the bag to see if there are other things that belong to us. If so, remove them and then put the canvas bag back under the tree. Hopefully, the remaining items will be returned to their rightful owners by the authorities. Okay? Go on, then." As the four backs of their friends faded into the darkness, David turned to Howard and said, "Let's pick up this piece of shit and put him in the trunk of my car. But we need to wait a few minutes for the others to leave in Steven's car."

It took fifteen minutes to drive to Whitcomb Woods. It was very dark, but David knew the area well. David pulled into a small lane bordering a corn field. He drove a quarter mile down the dirt road and then parked the car. The boys got out of the car and looked around. The night was quiet except for an owl hooting deep in the woods. After he was sure no one else was in the vicinity, David nodded at Howard and said, "Well let's get on with it."

David and Howard lifted the body out of the trunk. David grasped Joel's hands and Howard took hold of his feet. The moon had just gone into its waning stage, so there was sufficient moonlight for the boys to see as they carried the body deep into the woods.

David knew where there was a narrow ravine and whispered directions to Howard as they picked their way through the mixed forest of pine and deciduous trees. When they reached the edge of the ravine, the boys rolled the body down the slope. They picked their way down to where Joel Dalton's lifeless body came to rest. They covered the body with several fallen, large pine branches. Without a backward glance, they scrambled back up out of the ravine and trotted back to David's car.

The two friends were silent, caught up in their own thoughts as David drove back into town. David felt a little surprised that he'd felt no guilt for what they'd done. He rationalized it by reminding himself that he and his buddies were all drunk. They didn't mean to kill Dalton. It was an accident. Anyway, what was done was done. Going forward, he had to trust his fellow co-conspirators to keep the secret. He was relying on them to keep their mouths shut. *Would all four of them be able to keep the secret?* He was sure that he could. He had to! But the loyalty of his closest friends had never been tested to this extent. All four of them had so much potential. They had college to look forward to and challenging careers ahead of them! The death of a screwed-up, worthless, hillbilly thief could not ruin his or his friends' lives!

After he dropped Howard off, David reminded himself again. It was an accident. But he knew the authorities wouldn't just accept a boy's death at that. At the very least, he'd be arrested. Maybe his father could pull strings, or Robert Levitt could get him off ... but what would that do to his scholarship, and to his reputation? He'd be branded as a killer. No, the secret pact with his friends was the way to go. That was the only way to avoid terrible consequences for him and his friends.

As he lay in bed enduring a sleepless night, David thought about telling his father. He decided against it, because he believed his father would be upset, disappointed, and embarrassed by his son's stupidity and poor judgment. David knew his father's image of him was that of a bright, good, and loving son. He was the golden boy, the apple of Benjamin Weiss' eye. David couldn't bring himself to shatter that image. Even if he evaded a criminal conviction, his father would surely think him no longer worthy to someday run the Weiss Investment Group.

* * *

The following day, the group gathered at David's house. His father was traveling on business. The six friends sat out on the large screened-in porch facing the swimming pool. The members of the group were David, Howard White, Steven Mills, Angelina Mangano, Staci Lykaios, and Ann Gottlieb. All attractive, supposedly upstanding young citizens, sports stars, cheer leaders, honor students, and all college bound.

Angelina asked whether they ought to go out to the woods to inspect the body and make sure it was well hidden. That idea was quickly nixed by group acclamation. Steven didn't want to go anywhere near a dead body. More pragmatically, Howard pointed out that they should not draw unnecessary attention to Whitcomb Woods. After some further deliberation over the carry-out brunch Staci brought from her parents' restaurant, they all agreed once more to keep the secret and never discuss it with anyone else.

They agreed to stay alert and report back to the group, if there was any mention of Joel Dalton's disappearance in the local newspaper or television stations. Otherwise, they might not need to get together for any future discussions about what happened or what they should do.

Each of the six eighteen-year-olds believed they were acting correctly considering the circumstances. The close circle of friends agreed that they could trust each other to keep the secret, until it was no longer necessary. Before the meeting broke up, David pointed out that by keeping the secret they were all guilty of a crime. Each of them could be prosecuted, if they didn't keep their mouths shut. Howard chimed in to inform the group that there is no statute of limitation on murder.

Chapter 7

Six hours after Howard and David left Joel Dalton's body deep within the dense forest of Whitcomb Woods the sun began to rise. The morning dew slowly dissipated as the sun grew brighter. The branches that covered the body of Joel Dalton began to stir, and slowly Dalton woke up. He was cold, tired, hungry, and his body hurt all over. Dalton had taken the worst beating of his life the prior evening. The inside of his mouth felt dry and his saliva tasted unusually stale. He felt like he had to vomit. Dalton was unconscious most of the night. He had brief moments of semi-consciousness as he lay under broken pine branches and on top of a cushion of pine needles and forest debris. In those moments, he asked himself, *Am I dead or am I alive?* He didn't know until he was fully awakened by the sun spattering light across his face through the pine branches covering him.

He coughed, which partially cleared his throat. When he coughed again, phlegm and dried blood spewed out of his mouth. As his breathing began to improve, he noticed his jaw was not working properly and it hurt to open his mouth. But it was also difficult to breathe through his nose, because his right nostril was clogged with blood. Despite the pain and difficulty in breathing, Joel thought ruefully, *I probably should have died from that beating. I must be tougher than I thought. I'm still alive.* His chest, ribs, and gut, felt like a regiment of soldiers had marched over his body. At first, his memory was foggy about the details of what had happened to him. But as his head cleared, the events of the previous evening began to come into focus and ran through his mind like an action movie with a very bad ending.

Joel struggled to his knees and the pine branches fell off. He gasped for breath and more caked blood slid out of his nose. He whimpered in pain when he made the effort to stand on both feet. He almost fell, but managed to grab hold of a beech tree to steady himself. Joel looked around the woods. He had no idea where he was. He was afraid he would faint, he felt so weak. Another fear crept into his mind, how was he going to get home and how was he going to explain his injuries to his old man? In which direction would his father's volatile temper turn? Joel knew Lowell's reaction would be anger, but would he take it out on Joel or seek revenge on the guys that gave his son such a terrible beating.

Joel slowly stumbled along the base of the ravine using trees for support whenever he felt so weak, he thought he might fall. Eventually he saw a well-marked trail. And then he knew he was in the Whitcomb Woods. He knew these woods and the trails. Joel had spent many hours as a child exploring the woods and using the shelter of the forest as a hideout from his father. When he managed to plant his feet on the trail, he headed for home.

What Joel didn't know is that someone had been watching his progress from a distance. Since sunrise, a pair of eyes had observed Joel rise from the dead, gain his footing, and begin to trudge out of the forest. Joel's concentration was totally focused on coping with excruciating pain and putting one foot in front of the other in order to make his way home. He was unaware all of his movements were being scrutinized by the watchful eyes of a very interested observer.

When Joel finally entered the rundown house, he called home, he discovered that, thankfully, his father was not there. Another bit of luck was finding a large ham and cheese sandwich on a plate inside the refrigerator. Joel sat down at the kitchen table and devoured the sandwich. Despite the pain in his head, neck, and ribs, he felt surprisingly hungry. Next, he ate half a bag of barbecue potato chips and then gobbled down several chocolate chip cookies. He downed two cans of Diet Coke.

Joel was used to being dirty, but now he was really filthy. His black t-shirt was ripped and his black chinos were caked with dirt. Joel gingerly removed his clothes, and with a wrenching groan stepped into the shower. As warm running water cascaded over his battered and bruised body, he began to feel better. Joel rinsed the residue of blood out of his nose and left ear. He carefully dried himself off and then brushed his teeth. He left his dirty clothes and the wet towel in a heap on top of his bed. Joel eased his body into bed. He tried to sleep, but he had so many aches and pains he couldn't completely fall asleep.

Just when he was about to drift off, Joel heard a knock

on the front door. He slowly swung his legs over the side of the bed and peered out the window by his bed at the front porch. No one was at the door. Joel muttered a curse and began to ease his aching body back into bed, but then he heard gravel being thrown by the tires of a vehicle speeding away from the house. Joel lurched back to the window, but all he could see was a cloud of dust blown up behind a sedan tearing away down Quail Road. Joel didn't recognize the light-colored car because he could barely see it through the haze of dust still visible in the air.

Joel started to turn back toward his bed, but he noticed a white envelope lying on the front porch a couple feet away from the door. His curiosity was piqued, so, despite the pain, he made his way out to the porch. With a groan and a curse, Joel picked up the envelope. It had the Weiss Financial logo in the upper left corner. Inside were a lot of bills in varying denominations. Some of the bills were crispy, others looked worn, wrinkled, and old. Strangely, many of the bills had a stale odor. He counted the money and was amazed it totaled up to one thousand dollars. There was also a hand-written note on stationary. Joel's eyes widened as he read, "Keep your mouth shut about what happened last evening and get the hell out of Grassville right now or else." As he read 'or else' a pang of fear shot through Joel. This was serious. It was clearly a death threat.

Joel lowered his aching body onto a chair at the kitchen table. He had to think through his options. Despite the pain wracking his body, his mind was clear. The options were: 1. Keep the money, remain quiet, stay in town, and take your chances. 2. Report the assault to the authorities. 3.

Get out of town, as the note instructed. Joel Dalton prided himself on not being a snitch, but he wanted David Weiss and his buddies to pay for nearly beating him to death. He could tell Lowell and let his dad take revenge. But, after visualizing his father kicking the shit out of those preppies, he decided that would not be a very good move. Lowell might very well kill them. That could make things even worse.

The more Joel thought about it, the more attractive option number 3 seemed. Why not leave his father and Grassville for good? Now, he had the money to do what he'd wanted to do for a long time. If he decided to go, he wondered whether the authorities would be concerned about his disappearance. He could send an anonymous note to the police describing the assault. But, if the cops looked into it, he could be charged with breaking and entry and theft of all the stuff he stole out of the cars during the high school dinner/dance. After all, whose side were the authorities going to be on, the richest kids in Grassville or the hillbilly thief from the wrong side of town? Plus, if Benjamin Weiss decided to use his influence, nobody had a chance going up against such a powerful and respected member of the community. And, if the rumors were true about Weiss' connections with the Chicago mob, they might not bother with the law and just snuff him out.

It was decided. Joel took a cloth laundry bag hanging on a hook behind the bathroom door. He stuffed a clean pair of jeans, cut-off shorts, two t-shirts and a work shirt, two pairs of socks and underwear inside the bag. He snatched his toothbrush, a tube of toothpaste, and a razor out of the bathroom, along with a clean towel. He stuffed everything he thought he would need into the bag. Joel Dalton limped out of his house smiling to himself, even though every step he took down the unpaved, gravel surface of Quail Road was painful.

Joel realized that once the police were aware of his disappearance, there might be an investigation. If a crime was suspected, naturally, his father would be the prime suspect, because of Lowell's history of abusing Joel. The police might even accuse his dad of killing him and burying his body somewhere in Lawrence County. The thought of his father being wrongfully implicated in a crime brought a grin to Joel's bruised face. When he reached the main highway, Joel stuck out his thumb to get a ride. He might as well head toward the big city, Indianapolis.

He didn't have to wait long before a truck driver offered him a ride. The trucker asked about the bruises on Joel's face, but seemed satisfied with the explanation that he'd been in a fight over a girl at a school dance. The driver chuckled knowingly and let it go. The truck pulled off the road into a truck stop in Martinsville. The driver told Joel he planned to take a warm shower, get something to eat, and call it a day. As they exited the cab, the driver slapped Joel on the shoulder – which made Joel wince in pain – winked and said he'd pick up a whore for the night. "It's safer to pay for sex than have to fight for it," the trucker said with a laugh.

Joel grinned and started to walk the quarter mile back to State Road 37. Luckily, another trucker was just pulling out of the truck stop. He told Joel to hop in. Joel was dropped off on the south side of Indianapolis, near the I-465 interchange. Joel was too tired and sore to try to go any further for the night. It was a warm June night, so, using the laundry bag for a pillow Joel lay down under an exit ramp bridge. He immediately fell asleep to the relaxing sounds of vehicles whizzing overhead.

Joel's luck was not as good the second day on the road, but he was eventually picked up by a couple of Butler University students, who dropped him off in downtown Indianapolis by the Wheeler Mission on their way back to the BU campus. They told Joel he could get a shower, meal, and bed for the night there, because it was a homeless shelter.

Joel became a regular at the Wheeler Mission. He made connections with petty criminals staying at the mission. After he was accepted among the homeless lowlifes, Joel started asking around about finding a forger, who could make him a counterfeit ID. He was referred to a guy known as Slim, "the best fake ID man in Indy." Joel paid Slim $200 for a forged driver's license and a birth certificate. With his new identity, Joel began taking odd jobs and was able to move out of the homeless shelter and into a cheap apartment complex on the near east side of Indianapolis.

After the first beating he took at the age of five, Joel had dreamed about being free from his father. And now, he'd finally made it. "I'm free at last!" he shouted with glee inside his very own apartment the night he was given the key.

But the moment of joy was short-lived, because Joel

didn't feel completely free. Who had left the thousand dollars in the envelope? What did they know? Were they still watching him? Joel's best guess was that it was David Weiss. He had a clear motive, make amends for the beating and get Joel out of town so he wouldn't turn David and his friends in to the cops. But the light-colored older sedan wasn't David's vehicle. On the other hand, the envelope had the Weiss Financial logo on it. But anyone in Grassville with an account at the bank could have an envelope with the bank's logo on it. The note was unsigned, and he didn't know what David Weiss' handwriting looked like, so he couldn't be sure.

Joel decided he needed to try to let go of his nagging fears and suspicions. Whoever wrote the note and left the cash for him had done him a favor. The thousand dollars gave him the means to escape his father, their shitty little shack, and the life he hated in Grassville. He had a fresh start and could begin to live the life he'd dreamed about.

Chapter 8

At four-thirty a.m. on Monday, Sally Morgan, got up, took a quick shower, curled her bleached blond hair, and got ready to go to work. Morgan was Lowell Dalton's twenty-eight-year-old girlfriend. They'd had an on-again off-again relationship for a year. Prior to leaving her rented trailer in a rundown trailer park on the west side of Grassville, she ate an apple and a piece of toast with peanut butter. To feel fully awake she rinsed her food down with two cups of black caffeinated coffee. Sally stepped out of the trailer, locked the front door, and climbed into her rusty, 1981 Pontiac Le Mans.

Sally Morgan worked for Mangano Manufacturing. Mangano produced automobile parts. Sally's job was to package the products for sale to automobile part stores, like NAPA, all over the country. She worked first shift, which started at 6:00 a.m., Monday through Friday. Saturday and Sunday were reserved for shopping, dancing, drinking, and making love to Lowell Dalton.

Morgan was originally from Pennsboro, a little town in northern West Virginia near the Ohio/West Virginia border, about twenty miles east of Parkersburg, West Virginia on

State Highway 16. Sally grew up in a family of poor, but hardworking, coal miners. She could hardly wait to get out of Pennsboro. So, she applied herself to schoolwork and graduated with honors from Pennsboro High School. She was offered a partial scholarship to Ohio Valley University, a private NCAA Division II school in Vienna, West Virginia, not far from Pennsboro. Unfortunately, Sally couldn't afford to pay the balance of tuition and housing, so she was unable to fulfill her dream of going to college.

But Sally Morgan had an asset other than her brains, a killer body. She decided to utilize that asset to get out of Pennsboro. Her first job in a strip club was in Columbus, Ohio. After six months there, she received a more lucrative offer to dance at well-known strip club in Indianapolis, The Executive Lounge. "The Lounge" was located in downtown Indianapolis and was frequented by politicians, businessmen, out-of-town executives, and professional athletes. So, at the age of twenty-one Sally Morgan began performing in a club that allowed total nudity.

As the years passed, Sally put on some weight, smoked and drank too much, and didn't exercise, except for her 25 hours per week of erotic, nude dancing. She was still easy to look at, but years of hard living were beginning to show, along with the excess pounds. To supplement tips at The Lounge, Sally briefly tried her hand at prostitution. It lost its appeal after two arrests by vice cops and a beating by an abusive client.

Her stage name at The Lounge was Marilyn, because her body and hair resembled the late sex goddess, Marilyn Monroe. When she was on stage, Sally wore the same color of lip stick and nail polish, called ravishing red that Monroe famously wore. Her stage outfit was a filmy white robe, which set off the year-round tan Sally maintained with a tanning lamp. When Lowell Dalton saw her dance for the first time, he thought he was in love. But, for a man like Dalton there is little difference between a throbbing lust and love at first sight.

As their relationship developed, Sally told Lowell that she was in love with him too. But Lowell had a suspicious and paranoid personality and thought she was probably with him for drugs and cash. By the time Sally's career as a stripper ended, she had become a drug addict and an alcoholic. Lowell knew she liked the stuff he could provide, but wondered whether it was possible she also wanted him to be her permanent man. But with a drug-addicted stripper, like Sally, how the hell would he ever know? It was well known that strippers were masters of manipulation. Still, their relationship served both of their needs. Lowell asked Sally to move to Grassville, when she was fired at The Lounge. She hoped that maybe she could find a more normal life in Grassville. Maybe Lowell would be the one to provide it for her. Sally, however, did not know about Lowell's criminal history.

* * *

The previous Saturday night, after dinner and drinks at the Texas Roadhouse the couple returned to Sally's trailer for more drinking and pot smoking. Sally felt both high and amorous. She unbuckled Lowell's belt and pulled his zipper down to fondle his shaft. Lowell responded by completely undressing and hurriedly pulling Sally's clothes off of her. Their love-making was equally hurried and was over before Sally was fully satisfied. This was, however, the routine she'd gotten used to with Lowell. He was usually drunk when they had sex. He was overweight, abused drugs, and usually fell asleep by ten-thirty. But at least he was her man, Sally thought as she lay in his arms wide awake. She checked her alarm clock and it was ten forty-five p.m. Sally knew Lowell wouldn't wake up until at least nine a.m. on Sunday morning. *I've got to get up; I need to take care of something else.*

For his part, Dalton was happy to have Sally Morgan in his life for the time being. When they were passionate in making love, he liked to call her Marilyn, which increased his excitement just prior to climaxing. But Dalton was becoming increasingly worried about being able to keep up with her seemingly insatiable desire for sex. He knew he was getting older, but, *Man! How long will I be able to keep up this pace?*

Occasionally, Sally visited Dalton's home, which was just a few miles away from her trailer. But Lowell made it clear that he did not want her around his son, Joel. He was ashamed of his scrawny, worthless son, and besides, Joel had a big mouth. He'd get drunk or be stoned and talk about things he should not be discussing in front of her or anyone else. He even mouthed off about his latest scheme to join a crew of professional thieves from Bedford, Indiana to steal and fence farm equipment. *What the hell was my dumb ass son thinking to bring that up with Sally in the house?* Sally Morgan was just his girlfriend, not his wife. She wasn't family. Lowell sensed that Sally would like to marry him. He believed Sally was trustworthy and loved him in her own way. He was confident she wouldn't intentionally harm him. *But what if she was drunk or high and started flapping her jaw? She might say something to somebody that would come back to haunt him. Why would anyone want to take an unnecessary risk like that?*

* * *

Late Monday morning, Lowell Dalton awoke in Sally Morgan's bed. He finally rolled out of bed at ten-thirty a.m., put on his underwear and the rest of his clothes, relieved himself in the bathroom, splashed some cold water on his face, got into his pickup and returned to his own home on Quail Road. He immediately headed for the bedroom and flopped into bed. A weekend of vigorous sex with Sally left the forty-two-year-old all played out.

Lowell roused himself out of his own bed at two p.m. He went to the bathroom and then got a beer out of the refrigerator. He noticed there were dirty dishes lying in the sink and on the kitchen table. The neighborhood seemed unusually noisy for a Monday afternoon. He looked out the front window and saw some children happily playing outdoors. Their laughter, yelling, and screaming annoyed him. He muttered to himself grousing that those kids ought to be in school. But then he remembered that school was over for the year. *Huh! They're on summer break. No more school until the fall.* Dalton belched and then lowered his bulk into a chair to enjoy his cold beer.

Dalton was surprised that his son wasn't hanging around the house smoking marijuana, drinking booze, and watching television as was Joel's usual routine. After draining his beer, Lowell heaved himself up off the chair to look into his son's bedroom. He noted that Joel's bed had been slept in and the room was even messier than usual. The sheets were dirty and clothes were strewn all over the room. A wet bath towel was wadded up on top of the bed spread.

Strict rules Dalton had to follow in prison concerning proper hygiene had developed a surprising level of discipline in this otherwise very undisciplined man. The burden of housekeeping work, however, fell to Joel. Lowell assigned Joel the tasks of washing dishes, doing laundry, sweeping the floors, and making both their beds. Dalton considered himself generous to grant his son the privilege of a roof over his head, a soft bed, food to eat, a television, and not being hassled for doing drugs or drinking beer. Lowell reckoned that he'd given Joel a lot more than he had growing up in a crime-ridden neighborhood on the south side of Chicago.

Lowell was pissed off that Joel hadn't done his chores. *But what did I expect from that worthless son of mine? Wait until I get my hands on that kid. He knows better than to leave his room like that. I'll have to kick his ass a little harder tonight when he gets home.*

Since there was nothing, he could do about it now, and he certainly wasn't going to do the chores that were his son's responsibility, Lowell drank another beer and ate the rest of the pizza he'd left in the refrigerator on Friday. Dalton relieved himself again and went back to bed.

At six p.m., he woke up and listened for noises in the house. Hearing none, he got up and went out to the kitchen. The dirty dishes were still there and Joel had not yet returned home. *Where is that punk?* Joel should have been home by now complaining he was hungry. To be sure, Dalton was not worried about Joel's well-being or where he was. In fact, he hoped Joel was doing a job to bring in some money. *The little son of a bitch owes me.* He knew Joel would eventually show up. A sly grin creased Dalton's craggy face as he imagined Joel returning with boatloads of cash. But then he shook his head. *Fat chance that will ever happen in my lifetime.* Only in my dreams, he thought.

Since he didn't feel like making a meal just for himself, Dalton decided to go to the local tavern in downtown Grassville and get a double-cheeseburger, salty fries, and drink a few Pabst Blue Ribbon beers. Dalton took a quick shower, brushed his teeth, put on a short-sleeved shirt and a pair of jeans. He pulled on a scuffed pair of old cowboy boots and splashed some cheap cologne on his face. Always have to smell good for the ladies, Dalton told himself as he climbed into his rusty, late-model, pickup truck.

The usual crowd was at Charlie's Bar and Grill. Lowell's favorite waitress, one of the town sluts, Darlene French was serving at the bar. Dalton liked to flirt with Darlene, if Sally wasn't with him. He slid onto a bar stool and greeted Darlene with a broad smile and said, "Woman, you look good enough to eat. How 'bout I take you home and show you a good time?" Dalton winked at her mischievously. Darlene walked slowly toward Lowell. As she came around the bar, she arched her back to extend her already ample bust line even further. Lowell eyed her feminine curves appreciatively envisioning what she would look like naked.

Darlene leaned an elbow on the bar and looked up into Lowell's eyes with a seductive smile and said, "How's my handsome fella tonight? I see you didn't bring your girlfriend." Then she put her hand gently on his right thigh and gave it a soft caress. "So, does that mean we're finally going to get together?" She said in a sexy whisper close to Dalton's ear.

Dalton felt movement inside his pants, when Darlene gently squeezed his thigh. But it quickly wilted. The weekend with Sally had worn him out. He said in his most sincere voice, "You know honey, if you weren't working, I'd take you home right now."

"Well, don't let that stop you, big boy," Darlene replied teasingly.

Dalton chuckled, but looked away from Darlene feigning interest in checking out who else was at the bar. He was not about to tarnish his reputation as a ladies' man by admitting he didn't have the libido to lay another woman after a weekend of hot sex with his girlfriend. He liked to think he could screw every woman in town any day of the week. Although Lowell wouldn't admit it to anyone, he could feel that drive slipping away. But to keep up his act as the Don Juan of Charlie's Bar and Grill, he puffed his still-massive chest out and resuming a macho tone said, "One of these nights when you're not working, I'll show you how a real man treats a lady. You just be patient, and I'll prove I'm worth the wait." Dalton gave Darlene another sly wink.

Darlene stood up and resumed her role as waitress and bartender. She asked dryly, "What are you doing in town tonight, anyway? It's a Monday."

"I'm hungry and I wanted to have someone else do the cookin'."

"Well sweet heart, if you do me right, I'll cook for you every night," Darlene said mockingly, but with a little gleam in her eyes. Darlene doubted that Lowell would ever do more than posture as the big, sexy hunk – which he used to be. But she enjoyed their flirtations.

Lowell chuckled and replied, "One of these days you'll find out how good I can be to a woman." He leaned back and yawned. "I'm sure you've heard about my reputation."

Darlene laughed. "Oh, I've heard all about your reputation, but I'm beginning to wonder whether it's all show and no go," she said with a teasing smile. But before Lowell could mount another defense of his masculinity, Darlene changed the subject and asked patronizingly, "Since you're not gonna take me home to eat, what do you want to order? And, do you want a beer with your food?"

"My usual and an ice-cold PBR in a bottle." Dalton smiled with appreciation as Darlene's rump stretched her tight jeans to the limit, when she bent over the cooler to pick out a bottle of PBR.

She smiled brightly at Lowell as she slid the beer to him and said, "Give the cook a few minutes and I'll bring it right out to you, baby."

After consuming his double-cheeseburger and salty fries, several hours and many beers later, Dalton decided it was time to go home. It was just after ten p.m., when he weaved his way out of the bar. He hoisted his bulky body into the pick-up and drove back to his house on Quail Road.

Lowell lurched into the house and looked around. Joel had not returned. Dalton was half-drunk and it angered him that Joel still hadn't cleaned up the house. He would have liked to smack his son around. He didn't give a damn about his son's welfare or safety. But, if the little prick was gonna be out this late, he better be out trying to make some money. Dalton treated Joel like he was an indentured servant. The thought of calling the authorities to report Joel missing never crossed Lowell's mind. As Dalton stumbled off to bed, he comforted himself with the thought that he'd give Joel a good ass-kicking when he finally showed up – unless, he brought home a nice stash of stolen goods or a pile of cash. Then, he'd just smack his son a couple times.

* * *

Lowell's elderly next-door neighbor found it strange that he hadn't seen or heard from Joel Dalton for several days. Walter Sellers was worried. He liked the kid, felt sorry for him, and tried to keep track of him, as best he could. Over the years he'd shared a property line with Lowell Dalton, Walter had many times heard Joel's desperate pleas for his father to stop beating him. All of the neighbors on Quail Road knew Lowell Dalton was a terrible father. Lowell didn't try to hide the fact that he often beat Joel. And, all of the neighbors were afraid of Lowell's terrible temper. They knew he was a dangerous ex-con. Walter Sellers fretted that Dalton had finally done something horrible to Joel.

On Tuesday afternoon Sellers called the Lawrence County Sheriff's Office in Grassville to report that Joel Dalton was missing. Just as Lowell sat down to eat supper by himself, an officer appeared at Dalton's front door. Deputy Sheriff Billy Walters informed Lowell that he had questions concerning Joel's whereabouts. Lowell didn't let the Sheriff's deputy inside, but spoke to him through the open front door. Officer Walters asked Dalton where Joel was and why he hadn't reported his son missing. Dalton told the officer that Joel's whereabouts was none of his business. But when Walters kept asking questions about Joel, Lowell started getting nervous. So, as he always did when he started to feel cornered and couldn't use his fists to get out of the situation, he started lying. Lowell said that Joel was visiting his aunt in Vincennes, Indiana and would be back in a few days

Three days later, Deputy Sheriff Walters returned to check on Joel. He suspected Dalton had been lying to him, but didn't have any evidence to support his suspicions. Once again Lowell started obfuscating, so the deputy threatened to get a warrant. At that, Lowell finally admitted that the last time he saw his son was the prior Friday afternoon. Officer Walters told Dalton he needed to come in to the Lawrence County Sheriff's Department to fill out a missing person's report. If he refused, the deputy said things might get ugly and Lowell might get charged for a variety of crimes, like abandonment and child endangerment for starters. Dalton agreed.

When Dalton was seated in an interrogation room at the Sheriff's Department, a detective read his Miranda rights and began to question Lowell about his son. After five minutes of questioning, Dalton began to sweat and worried he was getting painted into a corner. *Holy shit*, he thought, *the cops think I've done something to Joel.* "I'm not gonna answer any more questions, unless I get to talk to an attorney," Lowell declared.

With that, the questions ceased, but it also confirmed in the detective's mind that Dalton was hiding something. In reality, Dalton had nothing to hide from the authorities, but he hated cops and he hated feeling pressured. *So, piss on 'em.* He didn't need to cooperate. He hadn't done anything wrong.

Ralph Harwich, the Sheriff Department's lead homicide detective, was conducting the interrogation of Lowell Dalton. Harwich was six-foot four-inches tall and built like an NFL linebacker. Most men were intimidated by Detective Harwich's size and stature. Lowell Dalton was not. Harwich knew Lowell Dalton was an ex-con, a notorious local hard-ass. When Dalton said he wanted to talk to an attorney, Harwich had to comply with the request. He said, "Okay, I'll get a court-appointed attorney to represent you." He stood up, told Dalton to wait while he secured an attorney, and would be back after the lawyer arrived.

Dalton pounded the table in anger when he heard the lock click after Harwich closed the door to the interrogation room. Dalton's anger and frustration mounted as time passed and he was trapped in the six by eight-foot room. After an hour of waiting, the attorney finally arrived. Dalton had no interest in discussing his missing son with the lawyer. Instead, he shouted furiously that the cops had deprived him of food, smokes, drinks, and the use of a bathroom. He said he was going to pee his pants, if he didn't get to a toilet NOW!

After Lowell was allowed to visit the men's room and the public defender had met privately with Dalton, counsel informed Harwich the interrogation could resume. When Dalton returned to the interrogation room, Harwich began to drill him again concerning the whereabouts of his son.

Dalton snapped back, "I've got no fucking idea where my son is!"

Considering Dalton's criminal record, his reputation as a local bully, and the history of accusations against him of beating up his son, Detective Harwich began to imagine the worst. He decided to try to draw Lowell out by "sharing a theory" with him. "Let's say you came home drunk, beat up your son, accidentally or intentionally killed him, and then disposed of his body. What would you say about my theory?" Harwich looked intently into Dalton's eyes as he waited for a response.

Up to their usual tricks – this is what the cops always do. They try to get you to confess to a crime you didn't commit. Ex-cons like me, they always try to shaft us. Dalton expected to be treated like he was guilty. In his mind, the presumption of innocence was an illusion. Cops always assumed he was guilty. "I'd say you are delusional, and you're out of your fucking mind. That's what I think of your so-called theory. I ain't intimidated by you or anyone else. I did nothing to my son. As I told you for the tenth time, I came home after a long weekend with my girlfriend, Sally Morgan, and Joel wasn't there. If you don't believe me, ask Sally. She can verify where I was the entire weekend, until I returned home late Monday morning. I have no idea where my boy is." Dalton stared angrily right back into Detective Harwich's eyes.

"Why, when, and where did you kill your son, Mr. Dalton?" Harwich calmly asked. Dalton might not be intimidated by his interrogator, but Harwich was not intimidated by Dalton's outburst. "What did you do with his body? Did you bury him, burn him up, cut him up, and then dispose of his body parts in various locations? Did you throw parts of him into the river, bury him in a shallow grave, or just torch the body?" Harwich asked in rapid fired questions. *Maybe Dalton's anger is his weakness. If I can exploit it, make him blow up, he might slip up and say something incriminating.* Harwich was not going to give up easily.

Dalton stared unblinking back at the detective and forced an evil grin onto his face. He shook his head, stroked his stubbled chin, pinched his lips together, and replied sweetly, "I don't know what you're talking about,

Detective."

Harwich knew his theory was pure speculation and there was no hard evidence to pin a crime on Dalton. It wasn't that unusual for boys from the "wrong side of town" with an abusive father to run away. After another half-hour of intense questioning, Wallace Brown, Dalton's defense attorney had enough. He told Harwich he'd have to arrest and charge Lowell with a crime or release him. Since there was no evidence of foul play, no body, and no witnesses to confirm anything sinister had happened to Joel, Detective Harwich was forced to let Dalton go free, at least for the present.

Brown assumed his client was guilty, because, during their private meeting, Dalton shared nothing about his missing son. The lawyer had advised his client of the attorney-client privilege, so that anything Dalton told him would remain confidential. But unbeknownst to the defense attorney or the detective, Dalton was trying to play them for a chance to sue Lawrence County. He'd been locked against his will in the interrogation room. He'd endured hours of interrogation for a crime he knew he didn't commit. He could play cat and mouse with the detective, until enough mistakes were made and his rights were violated to the extent the county would have to pay him compensation. Lowell Dalton was actually enjoying this little game. As to what had happened to his son, Lowell didn't really give a shit, but he was sure Joel would eventually drag his sorry ass back home.

Of course, Dalton knew he would be a suspect or person of interest, if Joel failed to reappear or failed to notify someone credible that he was still alive. As long as Joel was missing, whether the police could prove a crime had been committed or not, Dalton was going to be the most likely suspect. Most men would find that a very uncomfortable position. But, since that was the hand he was dealt, Lowell Dalton had decided he would try to turn it to his advantage.

The one kicker was that, with Joel out of the picture, Dalton would have to go back to work himself to bring in some money. By work, he didn't mean a legitimate job. No, Lowell Dalton was a career criminal, not anybody's gofer or employee. Lowell had taken note of what Joel told him about the experienced thief from Bedford, who had tried to recruit Joel into his crew. Joel said the crew stole tractors and farm implements, and fenced their bounty in Allen County, Indiana. With heat from the cops at present, Dalton knew it would not be a good time to get involved with a new gang, but the deal offered to Joel was definitely worth exploring in the future.

Chapter 9

A month later, Lowell Dalton couldn't resist the temptation to make some easy money. He decided to sell drugs to friends and acquaintances he trusted. Dalton knew the risks but thought limiting sales to people he knew would prevent him from getting busted. Unbeknownst to Dalton, one of his buddies, Drew Cole, ratted him out to the police. The cops caught his buddy with some weed and coke Dalton sold him. Cole already had a lengthy record. The quantity of drugs he was busted for constituted felony possession, so he was facing up to ten years jail time as a repeat offender.

Since Lowell Dalton was a known career criminal, the local authorities were anxious to get him off the streets, if they could nail him. With the information provided by Cole, it was clear Dalton was becoming one of the biggest drug dealers in Lawrence County. Cole introduced Dalton to a "trustworthy friend", named Wade Kline. What Cole didn't tell Dalton was that Kline was an undercover police officer with the Lawrence County Narcotics Task Force.

When Cole introduced Kline to Dalton, all Kline asked for was an ounce of pot from Dalton, and Kline offered to pay fifty percent higher than the going rate to prove good faith. Dalton agreed and then started making weekly sales to Kline. A month later, Dalton was under arrest. He had violated the terms of his parole and was charged with new felonies, possession, distribution, and racketeering. Lowell was convicted on all counts and transported back to his old home in the Indiana State penitentiary in Michigan City, Indiana to serve more time. Dalton's property on Quail Road was seized. According to State law, all of his personal property and the real estate were sold as fruits of his criminal activity at auction. The proceeds of sale went into the coffers of the State of Indiana.

While Dalton was in prison, he occasionally wondered what had happened to his son. He had never received notice that Joel was dead or that his body had been recovered. Dalton figured Joel was alive and well. *The kid had probably just left Grassville without leaving a trace.* They did have relatives in Vincennes, Indiana. Maybe Joel had hooked up with them. Out of curiosity Dalton called his sister Linda via the prison telephone system. She claimed she hadn't seen or heard from Joel since he disappeared. Lowell didn't think Linda would lie to him. She knew Lowell's temper, and what he'd do to anyone who tried to get over on him. Even though he was in prison, Linda was afraid of Lowell Dalton and what he would do to her, if she got caught lying to him.

Lowell was not worried about his son, but he needed someone on the outside to make connections for him. He wanted to supply drugs to inmates inside the Michigan City penitentiary. His plan was to develop a network using inmates' wives and girlfriends as couriers. The women could hide drugs in their undergarments, along with cash and other contraband, during their weekly visits. They could pass those items on to their boyfriends and spouses in return for a cut of the action from Lowell. But he needed a middleman to act as a go-between with his supplier and the women he'd draft into his network.

A monkey wrench in the plan was that Lowell was still under scrutiny for Joel's disappearance. That damn Lawrence County detective, Ralph Harwich, paid Lowell regular visits in the penitentiary to harass him about what prompted him to take his son's life and what he'd done with the body. Dalton continued to vehemently deny that he had any knowledge of what happened to his son. Harwich was a dogged investigator and was convinced Lowell knew more than he'd admitted about Joel's disappearance. But eventually Harwich had to accept that he hadn't shaken Lowell's claim of innocence and no new evidence had turned up to crack the case. After months as an active police file, the investigation of the disappearance and possible murder of Joel Dalton ground to a halt. Detective Harwich quit coming to the penitentiary to interview Dalton.

The Secret Pact

Chapter 10

Shortly after arriving in Indianapolis, Joel changed his name from Joel Dalton to George Nelson to conceal his identity. Since his two favorite entertainers were George Strait and Willie Nelson, Joel combined their names into George Nelson. He paid a forger two hundred dollars to create a fake Indiana driver's license and a Marion County birth certificate from Community Hospital East in Indianapolis. The birth date on the license and birth certificate was January 22, 1969. Joel applied for and received a social security card, which, he believed, cemented the credibility of his fake ID.

In the summer of 1988, Joel Dalton, now known as George Nelson, applied for an actual Indiana driver's license after taking a driving course at a driver-training academy. Even though he couldn't afford a vehicle, he was sure a real driver's license would come in handy. He was nineteen years old, and his new identification documents confirmed his age and his new name. Joel, aka George, looked younger than nineteen, because he was still skinny and looked under-nourished. But he was tall enough and never had a problem passing for George Nelson, age nineteen.

Looking to his future, George set his mind to achieving four goals: 1. To graduate from high school or obtain a GED. 2. To make lots of money and become rich. 3. To stop relying on crime for income. 4. To get a CDL license to drive a semi-truck.

George was technically a junior in high school, because, although he was nineteen years old, he had "lost" two years of school. He was twice sent away to a juvenile facility for six months on criminal charges. Because the courses taught in "juvey" were not up to the standards of Grassville schools, Joel was required to repeat the seventh and eighth grade. It pissed off Joel, but a "redo" of the seventh and eighth grades better prepared him for high school.

To accomplish his first goal, George Nelson went to a local agency that helped kids obtain a GED. But there was a problem. The agency asked for George's school records. How could he explain his new name? And, there was no way he was going to send for records from Grassville schools. He couldn't ask for help from his dad, because Lowell might come after him. When he learned he could get a GED without any school records, it would just cost more in fees for the preparatory courses, he thought the achievement program employees were ripping him off. But what could he do? George knew he'd never have a future better than a series of dead-end jobs without a diploma or a GED certificate. So, he paid the extra fees and took the courses.

George's first regular job was restocking shelves at a

run-down liquor store on the corner of North Meridian and East 14th street in downtown Indianapolis. The owner Paul Moretti, liked George; in part because George proved to be a hard worker, always on-time, and willing to work odd hours. Prior to working at Moretti's Meridian Liquor, George worked as a temp at various retail establishments, sweeping floors, cleaning bathrooms, unloading shipments, and stocking shelves, whatever it took to make a buck. When George wasn't putting in hours at the liquor store he hired out as a day laborer to earn additional cash. The day-labor jobs were usually hard, physical work on landscaping projects. But even with extra income from the day-labor work, George was barely making enough money to cover his living expenses.

Frankie Stenzi, the neighborhood drug dealer, lived two doors down from the apartment George rented. They became instant friends. Occasionally, George bought small amounts of weed from Frankie. Stenzi knew Paul Moretti, the owner of Moretti's Meridian Liquor, and helped George get hired. George worked nights and was paid $4.25 an hour in cash with no taxes withheld, but no benefits. He made about the same rate on day-labor jobs, unless it was extremely hard work, then he was paid another buck per hour. To get hired as a day laborer, George walked from his apartment to the intersection of Meridian and 38th Street and waited with a crowd of other men hoping to get chosen for a job.

George's work at Meridian Liquor began after the store closed for the day. The job required workers to be at least twenty-one-years of age, but Moretti hired him anyway based on Stenzi's recommendation. Stenzi told George to keep the job he'd have to do several things: 1. Keep his mouth shut about working there as a minor. 2. Not steal money or booze from the store. 3. Work hard and don't complain. George readily agreed. He worked a minimum of four hours, six nights a week restocking shelves. George liked the steady work. He wasn't saving any money, but with his income supplemented by day-labor jobs, George made enough to cover his living expenses.

Late one evening, Moretti told George that when he turned twenty-one, he would give George a regular job, not just restocking shelves, but also selling booze in the store and delivering beer, wine, and liquor to the wealthier patrons of Moretti's Meridian Liquor. He promised George that he'd increase his pay from $4.25 to $5.25 an hour and provide benefits when he became a permanent employee and took on the added responsibility. Moretti assured George that his hours would increase from twenty-four to forty hours a week.

George had not forgotten his goal of becoming a semi-truck driver. But he knew in order to become a commercial truck driver he'd have to get a CDL license and attend a truck-driving training school. CDL licenses were only issued to applicants that were twenty-one-years old or older, and George was fourteen months away from turning twenty-one.

Despite Frankie's warning, George occasionally stole a pint of booze from the liquor store, when Moretti wasn't looking. George usually ate at home in his studio apartment at the run-down apartment complex just off of E. Falls Creek Parkway N Drive on Hillside Ave. The complex was east of the Indiana State Fairgrounds. He bought cheap food, like macaroni and cheese, peanut butter, strawberry jam, bread, hamburger, eggs, cereal, fruit, vegetables, and milk. Joel drank a lot of water, but splurged on a liter of Diet Cola, when he had a few extra bucks. He bought most of his clothes from Goodwill.

Since he couldn't afford to buy a car as yet, George walked or rode a bicycle almost everywhere he went. Sometimes, he would take an IndyGo bus. Other than Frankie, George made very few friends. *Who needs them? So-called friends are just more unreliable people taking up space in my life.*

And despite his goal of making money without turning to crime, George started making drug deliveries for the one friend he'd made, Frankie Stenzi. Stenzi would give him "nickel" and "dime" bags of weed to deliver to some of his smaller clients. It took George several months to earn enough trust from Stenzi for Stenzi to allow George to start making bigger deliveries to more substantial clients. George knew he was backsliding on achieving his goal of leaving crime behind, but he was starting to make progress on his other goal of becoming rich. He was nowhere close to achieving actual wealth, but with full-time work at the liquor store supplemented by easy money as Frankie's delivery boy, George was actually beginning to save a little money each week.

George knew there was always risk involved working for a drug dealer. But, as a very small fish in the ocean of drugs sold in Indianapolis, George doubted that the authorities would be interested in him. In fact, Stenzi was not even on the radar of narcotics agents on the Indianapolis Drug Task Force. They were only interested in major dealers, and George's boss, Stenzi, was too small to bother with.

Working for Stenzi was easy. George kept small amounts of pot in his apartment. When Stenzi called to tell him where to make his next delivery, he did. Every other day, Stenzi came by the liquor store to collect his cash and give George his cut in weed or cash, whatever George preferred. Then, Stenzi would give George more grass to replace the stash he had already sold.

* * *

Articles about the disappearance of Joel Dalton ran occasionally in the Bedford Gazette, which was the local newspaper for Grassville, Indiana, for several months after he fled. The newspaper was available in the newspaper section of the main branch of the Indianapolis Public Library in downtown Indy, and George made sure to scope out the paper whenever he visited the library. George chuckled when he read that his father was a suspect in his disappearance. When he left home, George knew his dad would likely be the main suspect in the case. He wondered what his father was doing to replace the money he had provided on a weekly basis. He assumed his dad would either go back to selling drugs, stealing, or collecting gambling debts for the Indianapolis or Chicago mobs.

A few months later, he would read that his father had

been caught selling drugs to an undercover officer in Grassville. He knew his father would go back to prison. Lowell would have to serve the time remaining on his prior sentence plus whatever time was added for selling weed and cocaine. George couldn't help but feel a little sorry about his dad getting busted, but that feeling was tempered with thankfulness that he didn't get busted along with his dad.

George felt conflicted about his dad returning to the penitentiary. On the one hand, Lowell was a dangerously violent criminal. On the other, Lowell was still George's dad. George also thought that, while his father was going to prison for selling drugs, the authorities did not know half of what Lowell had done as a career criminal. It was well known that Lowell killed a man, supposedly by accident, but George knew that he had killed others for someone connected with the Indianapolis and Chicago mobs. Lowell never told Joel who the mobster was that he did hits for. He said it was none of his son's business. Lowell claimed that, if he ever told Joel his employer's name, it would be enough to get them both killed if the information got out. All Joel learned from his dad was that he occasionally worked for several mobsters, and he'd killed for them.

When Lowell was drunk, he sometimes bragged that he was a part-time problem solver for the mob. He carried a loaded small caliber revolver with him on his out-of-town trips. Lowell told his son that, if you carried a loaded gun, you had to be willing to use it. At six-foot two and two hundred eighty pounds of mostly muscle, Lowell didn't usually need to rely on a thirty-eight special for his defense. Joel Dalton was personally familiar with how lethal his father's fists could be, and he had no doubt that, with or without a gun, Lowell would be an effective killer for hire.

Chapter 11

Six weeks after his incarceration, Dalton got into a dispute with another inmate, who was a member of a Hispanic gang. The inmate that Dalton nearly beat to death with his fists and a cafeteria tray was connected to the Latin Kings, a well-known gang with ties to Indianapolis and Chicago. Lowell Dalton had messed with the wrong gang-banger. His victim was a cousin of the head of the Indianapolis "chapter" of the Latin Kings.

Several organized gangs, including the Aryan Brotherhood, tried to recruit Dalton into their prison gang. Many gang-bangers thought his talents would be a great addition to their organization. Being affiliated with a large gang, like the Brotherhood, would have afforded Lowell a great deal of protection. But he declined their offers and told them he could take care of himself. That turned out to be an unwise decision by Lowell.

Lowell Dalton was used to other men being afraid of him. He was a giant of a man and had a reputation for being an extremely tough fighter, half-crazy, a murderer, and just down-right mean. Lowell Dalton was someone you did not want to mess with in prison or anywhere else.

Dalton thought that, if any threat was directed against him in prison, he'd know ahead of time. He had his own network of friends, and he did favors for two prison guards. If and when the Latin Kings planned any retaliation, Dalton was sure he'd become aware of it. So far, he'd heard nothing. Dalton understood that no one can ever feel completely safe and secure in a maximum-security prison filled with more than two thousand dangerous men. There were plenty of treacherous inmates - like himself - in the Indiana State Penitentiary. Lifers had nothing to lose. What was the State going to do, if they shanked another inmate, give them a second life sentence? For many inmates, prison was the only life they knew.

On a Sunday morning after lunch, Dalton went back to his cell to take a short nap. It was raining heavily, so the inmates were not allowed out in the prison yard to exercise and socialize. Lowell had no idea that a designated Latin King assassin had given a hand-crafted shank to another inmate near Dalton's cell to hold.

At two p.m. the assassin received word that Dalton was asleep in his cell. The assassin retrieved the shank and slipped stealthily into Dalton's cell. He quickly confirmed that Lowell was asleep. The assassin leaped forward and planted his knee on Dalton's midsection, then stabbed him repeatedly in the chest. It happened so fast Dalton couldn't defend himself. He was just starting to wake up as the blade pierced his chest the first time. Before he was fully conscious Lowell Dalton was stabbed seven times, twice in the heart.

Not one of the prisoners in Dalton's cell block raised an

alarm to let the staff know what happened. They remained quietly in their cells. But twenty minutes after he was dead, a guard making his rounds in the block discovered Dalton's bloody body. He raised the alarm, and the entire prison population was locked down inside their cells.

Dalton's assassin, Jorge Gonzalez, was a professional. He worked the shank so quickly and precisely, not a drop of Dalton's blood stained his prison uniform. After the deed, Gonzalez slipped back into his cell before the alarm sounded and all the cell doors were locked.

The authorities did not know who committed the murder, but they were certain the Latin Kings ordered the hit. All of the inmates in cells near Dalton's were questioned by the authorities. Unsurprisingly, not one of them heard anything or knew anything.

However, three days after the murder a snitch inside the cell block deposited a note into what the inmates referred to as a "snitch box". Inmates use the snitch boxes to pass information about other inmates on to the authorities in hopes of the reward of an early release or special privileges. The boxes are locked and made of hardened steel and stored in a safe and secluded location inside the prison walls. But first-time snitches soon discover that once they've become informants, they will have to cooperate fully or risk being exposed. And, known snitches don't last very long in the "gen pop", the general population.

The note left in the snitch box informed the authorities that an inmate, who occupied a nearby cell to Dalton's, had hidden a shank inside his cell. The day of the murder, Jorge

Gonzalez retrieved the shank from that cell and used it to kill Dalton.

Dalton's closest relatives were notified within twenty-four hours after he was murdered. None of his relatives indicated they would attend the services scheduled for Lowell in the prison chapel. Of course, there was no way to inform Joel Dalton his father was dead. The authorities believed that Lowell was responsible for Joel's fate, whatever that was. If Joel was alive, he probably had no knowledge of his father's incarceration or his demise. If Joel had seen a death notice in any of the newspapers who printed it, would he want to come to the prison funeral service or burial of his dad? Unlikely.

* * *

When the story broke in the Bedford Gazette that his father was murdered in the Indiana State Prison in Michigan City, George was saddened but not surprised. Should he go up to Michigan City for the service and to say his last goodbyes? No, he couldn't risk blowing his own cover. George's feeling of sadness was mixed with relief due to his father's demise. Lowell was gone for good. He had to accept that, but he would also have to live with the psychic damage Lowell had done to him.

* * *

Lowell Dalton was buried in a small cemetery plot just outside the penitentiary walls. The cemetery was maintained by the prison staff and owned by the state. The warden provided a cheap wooden casket for Dalton's body, since he was indigent. A wooden cross and a metal plaque manufactured in the prison's industrial training center by the inmates marked Lowell's grave.

One person had attended Lowell's funeral and burial, his girlfriend, Sally Morgan. Sally went to the closed-casket graveside service to pay her last respects to the remains of the man she loved. She wore a black dress, black high heels, and a black lacy funeral veil to cover her face. Sally wept during the services and briefly after they concluded.

The prison minister who officiated at Lowell's funeral introduced himself to Sally at the end of the services. Pastor Art Lawson graciously expressed his condolences for her loss and told her Lowell was now with God forever. He assured her God was a loving God and would forgive Lowell for his sins. Sally doubted that. Lowell never went to church and had no interest in religion.

Sally watched in tears as her former lover's casket was lowered down into the hole and covered with dirt. She placed a bouquet of flowers on the freshly covered grave. Sally stood beside Lowell's grave gazing at the marker for several minutes. When she walked away from the cemetery brushing away the last of her tears, Sally Morgan was sure that she would never return to the Indiana State Penitentiary graveyard.

As days passed after the funeral, Sally became

extremely depressed. Now that she knew she would never see him again, it hurt deeply to realize how much she loved and missed Lowell. Sally was a functioning alcoholic and a recreational drug user while Lowell was alive. But without the coping skills to deal with the traumatic passing of her lover, Sally sank lower and lower into the pit of despair. She hardly ate. All she did was sit around her trailer, drink booze, and do drugs.

Several weeks after Lowell's funeral, Sally went on an amphetamine binge and tried to kill herself by ingesting too many pills. The overdose might have killed her, if a concerned next-door neighbor had not stopped by to check on her. She found Sally lying on the floor unconscious and about half dead. The neighbor immediately called for an ambulance. The EMTs arrived in time to save Sally's life. Sally spent a couple days in the hospital's ICU and was then transferred to the psychiatric ward for her own protection. A psychiatrist was assigned to evaluate Sally's condition. He determined she was border line psychotic and clinically depressed. She also had a severe substance abuse problem and was a danger to herself. Several weeks later, the Lawrence County Circuit Court judge ordered the Sheriff's department staff to transport Sally Anne Morgan to the psychiatric care facility in Logansport, Indiana, for long-term care and treatment. While Sally was driven to Logansport secure inside a police van medicated and confused, her only coherent thought was that nothing really mattered to her anymore.

* * *

After leaving Grassville, George had time to reflect on his father's past. His dad grew up tough, in a crime ridden neighborhood in South Chicago. *I guess he repeated his very harsh upbringing on me. Was he a good father or friend! No, but he didn't know any other way. Not that it wholly excused my dad for the way he treated me, but I guess his own upbringing made him into the man and father he was.* After much soul searching and reflection, George knew he had to forgive his dad and move on with his life. After all, Lowell was his father, even though he was not a good one. In spite of all the abuse he'd suffered at his father's hands and the problems it had caused being Lowell Dalton's son, he had to let it go and, in some sense, forgive his dad. It was time to forget the past and write the next chapter in his life.

George now felt both truly free to chart his own course in life and truly alone. His mother, Sarah, had deserted him when he was so young, he could barely remember her. And now his father was gone too. He was the only surviving member of his dysfunctional family. He thought, *I am now totally responsible for myself.* But he also understood that was what growing up was all about. Even though it was something he'd dreamed about for a very long time, being on his own was hard and demanding. With the death of his father, George realized he was entering a new stage in life and he had to prepare himself to face the coming challenges.

The Secret Pact

Chapter 12

Prior to leaving Grassville, Saul Workman told his wife Anne the reason why they had to sell their home and leave town. He said he had foolishly quit his job over a salary dispute. Workman purposely failed to mention to Anne that he was caught stealing money from Weiss Financial and had been fired and escorted out of the bank. Instead, Saul told Anne that he had subscribed to a service that provided salary information for similarly sized banks to Weiss Financial. The morning he quit his job, he had read a comparison study and was surprised by the disparity between his salary and the average salary for the same position at other banks. His salary was appreciably lower. Since he had received many citations and awards for his outstanding performance, he felt betrayed by his employer. Saul said that he requested a meeting with Robert Levitt, the Chief Operating Officer for Weiss Financial. He wanted to discuss the salary comparison study, and ask for a raise. "Unfortunately, during the conversation with Levitt I lost my temper and told him I'd quit, unless he immediately gave me a thirty percent raise. Honey, I guess I over-played my hand, because Levitt told me he accepted my resignation right then and there."

Anne was not shocked. The same scenario happened earlier in her husband's career. Saul was usually a calm and rational person, but when he thought he was being treated unfairly, well, it seemed to unleash some demons he ordinarily managed to suppress. He'd lose his temper, if he thought he was being screwed over by a superior. And then, he'd lose his job.

Saul explained to Anne that, when he lost his temper, the conversation with Levitt spiraled out of control. "I never should have demanded a thirty percent raise, but I didn't think Levitt would react like he was personally insulted. But after I said I'd quit, I couldn't take it back, could I?"

Anne shook her head sympathetically and held Saul's hand as he went on. "Well, after I exploded, I knew I'd screwed up and it was too late to expect another chance from Levitt. His face turned red and he said it was Weiss Financials' practice to accept resignations immediately once given. And that was that. He told me to clean out my desk and leave." Saul told Anne that his co-workers in the branch were stunned when they saw him walking out the door.

The fact that Robert Levitt stood watching Saul Workman with his arms crossed while Workman cleaned out his desk, and then Levitt escorted Saul out the back door did stun the other bank employees. They wondered what Saul had done so wrong as to be fired on the spot. Nobody in middle or upper management had a clue as to why Workman was peremptorily dismissed, except Levitt, Peter Adkins, the auditor, and Benjamin Weiss, the owner.

The whole thing was very unusual. After all, Workman had been employed for ten years by Weiss Financial as a senior branch bank manager.

Two weeks after Workman's termination, Levitt gave Kristine Sawyer, his trusted executive secretary, a few days off. Betty Turnbow, an office clerk, was picked by Levitt to take temporary charge of Sawyer's responsibilities. Betty Turnbow was by nature a very inquisitive person. It was common knowledge among the top executives in Weiss Financial that she could not be trusted with sensitive information. And that is exactly why Levitt selected her to fill in for Sawyer. Many of Turnbow's co-workers wondered why Levitt picked her for the temporary job. What they failed to consider was that, if you wanted information to get out, which Levitt did, you'd be sure to tell Betty Turnbow. She was the self-appointed head of the Weiss Financial rumor mill.

The following morning, Levitt purposely left his office door cracked open, picked up the receiver, and pretended to make a phone call to Benjamin Weiss. He actually dialed his home phone number and spoke into the receiver as if he was talking to Benjamin Weiss. He paused at the appropriate times during the fake conversation. In reality, his words were being recorded on his answering machine. The "conversation" began with Levitt supposedly greeting Weiss. Levitt then told Weiss that Workman had quit over a dispute they had concerning his last salary increase. Saul Workman insisted that his salary was not satisfactory. The fake conversation continued with Levitt telling Weiss that Workman got very angry and decided to quit. Levitt said in a sympathetic tone that after shouting and demanding a thirty percent raise, Workman started to calm down claiming his ego got the better of him, because he felt hurt when he learned he was under paid compared to other branch managers. "But seeing him lose his temper and shout at me within the hearing of other employees, well, when Workman said, 'I quit', I felt like I had no choice but to require him to leave. So, I told Workman that his resignation was accepted."

Betty Turnbow's ears perked up when she heard Saul Workman's name mentioned by Levitt, and she strained to hear the entire "conversation" Levitt was having with Benjamin Weiss. At the next coffee break, Betty relayed what she'd heard to the rest of the office staff, who listened to her gossip in rapt attention in the break room. The word was out. Workman had not been fired. He quit his job over a salary dispute and Levitt accepted his resignation.

A week later after the fake conversation, Levitt called his contact in Chicago, Jimmy "The Fist" Perilli. Perilli acquired his nickname, "The Fist", because he had killed several people with one punch. If you got hit by Perilli and lived, you'd never forget it. But more likely, you'd have no memory of it, because you'd be dead. Perilli had worked for Weiss on a few other jobs, so he knew what to expect when he got the call from Robert Levitt. After Levitt informed Perilli of what he was expected to do, Levitt ended the conversation saying, "We've done our part, now the rest is up to you." After he hung up the phone, Levitt drove to the Post Office and mailed a recent photograph of Saul Workman to Perilli. Levitt told Perilli he would be advised of Workman's address after Workman moved and resettled somewhere outside of the Grassville area.

It only took a month to sell the Workman residence, which was an immaculately kept, 1,800 sq. foot three-bedroom home in Bedford, Indiana. Their new address was on Worthingham Road in Chagrin Falls, Ohio, a village with a population of 4,000. Two weeks later the sellers accepted Saul's offer on the Worthingham Road property. During the transition and moving stages, Saul's family stayed in Uncle Maury's home in Cleveland.

Following the closing on his new home, Saul instructed Weiss Financial to transfer the remaining balances in his checking and saving account to his new bank in Twinsburg, Ohio. Fortunately, Saul had quickly found a job as an assistant branch bank manager at the United Bank of Twinsburg. It was a convenient fifteen-minute commute from his home in Chagrin Falls. The bank was a branch of a regional Ohio banking corporation, The United Bank.

The couple decided to move to Ohio after visiting Uncle Maury's home in Chagrin Falls to prepare the property to be sold. Maury assumed he wasn't going to live much longer due to his diagnosis of incurable pancreatic cancer. His oncologist agreed with Maury's assumption. Anne and Saul liked what they saw when they drove into Chagrin Falls. The upscale suburban community was close to Cleveland. The Workmans appreciated the advantages large cities offer. Anne was pleased their son Johnny would be attending an excellent elementary school in Chagrin Falls.

Uncle Maury wanted his favorite nephew to move closer to the Cleveland area, so he could spend some quality time with him before he passed away. So that made the decision to move to Chagrin Falls an easy one. Plus, Maury had offered to let the Workmans use his home, rent free, as long as they needed to, at least until he died. Maury's last will and testament specified that the house would be sold by his estate. Saul told Anne that Uncle Maury was going to leave them a small fortune of mostly liquid assets. That was all Anne needed to know to be on board with the move.

* * *

At three a.m. on Sunday morning Saul Workman's telephone rang nosily. He was drowsy from a Saturday night of drinking and dancing with Anne. He removed his arm from her around her waist, rolled over, picked up the receiver, and mumbled, "Hello."

"Hi," said the caller. This is Jane Hyatt calling from Intercity Security. I know it's late but there is a problem at the Twinsburg Bank."

"I'm not interested in a security system," Workman replied irritably. As he started to hang up the phone to go back to sleep, he heard the caller's voice pleading, "Don't hang up on me, please. I need to talk with Saul Workman. Is that you?"

He answered gruffly, "Yes, I'm Saul Workman. What's the reason for calling so early in the morning?"

"Sorry for waking you up this early, Mr. Workman, but the alarm system at the Twinsburg branch bank has gone off and we need someone to reset the alarm and open the bank for the police. The police are at the bank now, waiting for you to let them in."

Saul remembered that he was on call for emergencies this weekend, so he collected his wits and replied, "Okay, give me about thirty minutes and I'll be there. I just need to wake up, put on my clothes, and drive to the bank. Thanks for the call ma'am." He hung up the telephone and then looked over at Anne. She had gone back to sleep after briefly awaking to the annoying sound of the phone ringing. Workman admired her naked form for a second, then kissed her shoulder and smoothed over her brunette-colored hair with his hand. They had enjoyed making love late Saturday night. *I wish our relations could always be as passionate as they were last night*, he thought as he rolled out of bed.

Twenty-two minutes later Workman arrived at his branch of the Twinsburg Bank. A police car was parked in the small parking lot in front of the bank. Two uniformed officers were inside the vehicle. The officer in the front passenger seat waved at Saul to come over, and then told him to get into the back seat to fill out an incident report. As soon as Saul closed the door of the police car, a large man appeared outside the police cruiser and reopened the rear passenger door Saul had just closed. He was not wearing a uniform. The huge man bent down and poked a beefy face through the open door. He squinted carefully at Saul. The powerfully built man with huge shoulders and biceps that strained to break through his dark suit coat nodded at the uniformed officer in the front passenger seat. The cop pulled a gun, pointed it at Saul, and told him not to panic. Then, he handed Saul a black pillowcase and instructed him to put it over his head. Saul complied with shaking hands.

Saul's mind raced. He gulped and trembled. *This must be a robbery, but why do they need a hostage? Why me? Do they think because I'm a banker, I'm rich? Did they know about Uncle Maury's estate?* When Saul was calm enough to control his breathing, he asked what was going on and explained that he could let them into the bank, if that's what they wanted. No response. Saul kept a grip on his nerves and went on, "I don't have the combination to the safe. Only the manager and regional supervisor have it." Finally, a response; he heard the driver say, "I guess we'll have to use Workman as leverage on Monday morning when the bank manager opens the bank." Then he heard the gruff voice of the big man who had shoved Saul over as he shouldered his way into the car say, "I guess you're right, but we'll see." Workman noted that large man had an Italian accent.

The big man leaned across the seat and tied Saul's hands and feet with plastic ties. He reached into Saul's coat pocket and pulled out his car keys. He secured the pillowcase over Saul's head with a string and told Saul to lie down on the floor of the car. A minute later, Saul felt the patrol car moving. "What do you want from me?" he squeaked. "I have money, if that's what you want!" Saul could feel panic rising in his gut.

The big man rested his feet on Saul's curled up legs, and grunted, "Keep your mouth shut and do exactly as we say and you'll be alright."

"I appreciate knowing that but my wife will be worried and will probably call the police if I don't return home fairly soon." Saul hoped that might convince his captors to let him go.

"I guess we'll have to deal with that situation too," the driver retorted.

Saul wondered what that meant. Saul tried to surreptitiously loosen the ties that bound his hands. But his efforts just made the plastic tie dig painfully into his wrists. Out of frustration and anger, Saul began to scream, "Help, help!"

The driver quickly pulled over and stopped the car. He turned to the back seat and said, "Listen to me very carefully, Mr. Workman. If you don't relax and shut the fuck up, my partner is going to put a bullet in your head. Then, we'll drive over to Worthingham Road and visit Anne and Johnny. Do you want me to tell you what I'm going to do to them, if you don't cooperate?"

Saul sobbed, but quit screaming. What had he done to deserve this? How did these men know all about him and his family? If this wasn't a bank robbery, who had he pissed off so badly they hired these men to kidnap him? Saul thought maybe it was Weiss or Levitt getting back at him for stealing money from the bank. But wasn't that over? He had complied with their requests and paid the money back in full. He'd moved as requested and complied with all their instructions. Levitt told him they were square. *What the hell is this all about?*

After a twenty-minute drive, the vehicle stopped and both "officers" and the big man got out of the car. Several minutes later a rear passenger door was opened and Saul was hauled out of the car. Workman tried to determine where he was, but he couldn't see anything through the covering. He could hear the faint sound of an occasional vehicle going down a roadway, but he couldn't tell how far he was from the road. He smelled a foul odor. It reminded Saul of the smell of dung from a hog farm. He concluded they were out in a field in a desolate farming area. All of a sudden, a pair of large hands grabbed Saul and dragged him across a rugged field. He could hear the sound of water moving, probably from a small creek.

Saul began to think he was going to be killed. He held out a shred of hope that he was just being hauled off to a hiding place and this was a kidnapping for ransom. *What the hell do these fake cops and the giant want from me? I offered to give them access to the bank and I offered them money. What else could they want?* Saul began to panic again and started screaming for help. A hard punch to his gut silenced him. "We told you to keep your mouth shut," the voice with the Italian accent said. Workman's bowels let go and he peed his pants. He involuntarily let out another scream. A second punch landed on his jaw and broke it. Through ringing ears, Saul heard a voice say, "I think we're close enough." They stopped walking and one of the men propped his shaking body up and held him in an erect position. Workman tried to struggle, but he felt like he was frozen in time.

Pirelli attached a silencer to a twenty-two semi-automatic pistol. He paid no attention to Workman pleading for his life. The words, "I've got a wife and a young son, please let me live," had no affect on his professional demeanor. Neither did Saul's final pleas broken by sobs. There was a muted blast and Saul Workman was dead. His body collapsed onto the ground. Pirelli fired another bullet into the right side of Workman's head and then emptied the clip into his upper torso.

The two fake cops dragged Workman's body to a shallow hole they had previously dug. They removed Saul's clothes and pushed the body into the hole. Next, they poured lye over the corpse and then covered it with dirt. They drove the police car to another location, abandoned the vehicle, and then torched the car. At the same time, Workman's 87 Lexus was being taken to a salvage yard on the west side of Cleveland. It was compacted into a four by four-foot cube by an automobile crushing machine.

Early that evening, Levitt received the expected call from Perilli. All Perilli said was, "It's done. No problems. Thanks for the work."

Levitt immediately called Weiss. All he said was, "It's done, Boss."

The only thing Weiss said to Levitt was "good job" and then they both hung up their phones.

* * *

Early Sunday afternoon, Anne Workman called the Chagrin Falls police station and reported her husband missing. The police invited her to come to the station and fill out a missing person's report, but advised her that she might be acting a bit hastily. At the station a desk officer told her it was too early to file the report and that it was policy to wait at least two days before filing the report. But Anne explained the strange circumstances of her husband being called to the bank by the bank's security firm, and so she was allowed to fill out a report. Anne had a way of getting what she wanted. Her natural beauty and shapely figure probably helped persuade the male cops manning the desk.

Detective Michael Raines was assigned to the case. Anne filled him in on the early morning phone call Saul received. She said she overheard a conversation with a woman, who identified herself as a dispatcher for Intercity Security. The dispatcher told her husband that there was a problem at the Twinsburg Bank. He was being summoned by the dispatcher to reset the burglar alarm that had gone off at the bank branch where Saul was the assistant manager. Anne said she overheard the caller tell her husband that the police were waiting for him at the bank. Apparently, the police wanted access to the inside of the bank to check it out and make sure everything was alright. Anne gave officer Raines a description of Saul's red 87 Lexus sedan and the license plate number.

Detective Raines politely thanked Anne for the information. Raines assured her the police would look into the matter and see if they could develop any leads. Anne told him that they had recently moved to the area and had no enemies, as far as she knew.

Raines initially suspected that Saul Workman had a girlfriend and had run off with her, but after spending an hour with Anne, he discounted that theory. He told his supervisor in confidence that, if he was married to Mrs. Workman, he would never leave her. He described Mrs. Workman as being quite considerate, easy to talk to, polite, and extraordinarily attractive. That foul play was involved seemed more likely after the detective learned that no officers had been dispatched to the bank early Sunday morning and Intercity Security had no record of an alarm going off at the bank. Raines called Anne and asked her to come back to the station for further questioning.

When Anne mentioned in the follow-up interview that her husband was going to receive a sizable inheritance from his uncle, Raines wondered if Anne might be in league with others to grab the fortune just awaiting Uncle Maury's death. But he doubted that theory too. He had interviewed her extensively and determined that Mrs. Anne Workman was not the criminal type and certainly was not a murderer.

As subtly as he could, Raines tried to probe to discover whether Anne might have become angry at her husband and paid someone to get rid of him, Anne immediately volunteered to take a lie detector test to prove her innocence. She passed with flying colors. So, Detective Raines told Anne that, since there were no witnesses, no body, and no one else to pursue, they would have to continue the investigation. He advised her to be patient and that he'd get back to her if he had any more questions for her. Detective Raines encouraged Anne to call him, if she thought of anything else that might be helpful to the investigation.

Anne Workman was frightened and worried. She doubted that Saul would ever cheat on her. Whatever faults he had, he was a devoted father and husband. She was sure he would never leave her and their son Johnny to run off with another woman. Anne loved Saul, and she realized with bitterness how deeply she loved him now that he was missing.

Detective Raines feared Saul's missing person case would be a hard case to solve, but he didn't mention that to Mrs. Workman. The deeper Raines got into the case the more worried he became that Saul Workman was abducted, murdered, and buried out in the middle of nowhere. So far, no evidence turned up indicating Saul was still alive. What puzzled the detective was that neither Mrs. Workman nor any of the employees at the bank, where Saul worked, were aware of anyone who wanted him dead.

Chapter 13

With the Joel Dalton situation behind them, David Weiss and his friends prepared for the next big step in their lives – to attend college. College life for David was going to be hectic. It started in May 1988 with summer football camp on the Indiana University campus. First, each new member of the team was photographed and interviewed for the IU 1988-89 Football Season Preview magazine. In mid-May, David and other members of the team in the "skill players" positions attended an IU Booster Club luncheon. Coach Mallory personally introduced the freshman quarterback to important members of the Booster Club; one of whom was well known to David, his father, Benjamin Weiss.

Benjamin Weiss was delighted that his son decided to play for the IU football team. He attended every one of David's high school games, so long as business didn't take him out of town on a Friday evening. When Coach Mallory introduced David as the newest addition to the quarterback squad, during the luncheon, Benjamin Weiss beamed with pride. And, he stood and clapped along with the rest of the supporters, when Coach Mallory said David was expected to be number one on the QB depth chart. When his son stood at the podium and introduced himself, Benjamin shed a few tears.

Benjamin Weiss gave much of the credit to Miriam Gleiser, David's nanny since birth, for molding David into the fine, young man he had become. Weiss took great care in selecting Miriam to raise his son, and he trusted her completely. Neither Benjamin nor Miriam ever revealed to David that from 1955 to June 1957 they were lovers. Years earlier, both Weiss and Gleiser were employed at Benjamin Weiss' great-uncle's bank. That's where Benjamin learned the banking business, under the wing of his grandfather's brother, Howard Weiss, who owned a bank in Manhattan.

Miriam was a loyal and dedicated employee of the Weiss Bank of New York. She was attractive, intelligent, talented, and able to deal with difficult and important clients. Benjamin was impressed with her and attracted to her. Miriam worked tirelessly to make sure the bank's wealthy clients were provided excellent service and whatever financial needs they had; they were accommodated. Miriam was not married.

Miriam's father was a railroad conductor in pre-war Germany. Because Heinz Gleiser and his family were required to move frequently by the railroad, the Nazi persecution of Jews never targeted them. The Gleisers were never anywhere long enough to plant roots and join a synagogue. Unlike many other German Jews, Heinz foresaw the dangers Jews were going to face from the Nazi's before Kristallnacht. So, he hid their Jewishness by attending Catholic mass instead of worshiping at a synagogue. But, despite these precautions, both of Miriam's parents were eventually caught by the Nazi's and died in the gas chambers of Dachau. Miriam managed to escape Germany by using false identification papers based on the true identity of a deceased Catholic friend, who was the same age. She survived the Holocaust and managed to immigrate to the United States at the end of World War II as Marie Wegener.

Miriam and Benjamin's relationship came to an end on May 27, 1959. Benjamin met and started dating Vanessa Goldberg in July 1957, and they were married on May 28, 1959. The night before the wedding, Benjamin told Miriam their affair was over. He told her that he would be true to Vanessa until his dying day. Miriam was heartbroken that Weiss picked Vanessa over her, but what could she do? He had been honest with her. He told her he was seeing another woman, when he started dating Vanessa. Benjamin always treated Miriam with respect. So, Miriam decided she would remain loyal to Benjamin, and, as to the future, he could use her services as he chose to.

David knew his father liked Miriam, but he had no idea how deep and far back their relationship went. Miriam was David's mother for all intents and purposes other than carrying him in her womb. David secretly wished that his father would marry Miriam, but he never expressed his wish to either of them.

Vanessa died during childbirth. She was only twenty-two years-old. Despite Benjamin's vow to love only Vanessa to his dying day, his relationship with Miriam reverted back to the way it was prior to his marriage. Five months after Vanessa's death, their passion was rekindled. Benjamin Weiss was lonely and depressed. Miriam's solace was a comfort to him. Benjamin had assumed he'd die before Vanessa did. She was a healthy young woman, who didn't have the stress and burden of running a business with clients like the Perilli crew in Chicago.

The Perilli's were good customers of Weiss Financial. They relied on the bank to launder the money they made off their illegal enterprises. The Perilli crew was headed by two brothers, Jimmy (The Fist) Perilli and Joe (Little Joey) Perilli, Jimmy's younger brother. They were a branch of the Altobello crime family known as "The Outfit", the most powerful mafia family in the Midwest. Bruno Altobello sat on the mob's national commission in New York City, along with the capos of the other families. The Commission was originally chaired by Charles "Lucky" Luciano, and it controlled organized crime in the United States for two generations.

Benjamin Weiss and Jimmy Perilli were in the same neighborhood gang when they were just young punks on the Lower East Side of Manhattan in the early 1940's. Although their lives were set on very different tracks after they grew up and left NYC, a lifelong bond had been forged. One day Perilli contacted Weiss for a favor. Perilli was making so much money in the Chicago rackets his usual sources couldn't effectively launder all of it. So, he contacted his old friend, Benjamin Weiss, for help to launder money for him "on a temporary basis". Weiss felt obligated, so he granted Perilli the favor with the understanding it would just be temporary.

Perilli was so pleased with the clever way Weiss handled the transaction, he asked Benjamin to take on his crew's business long-term. He offered to do all of his legitimate, and illegitimate, banking with Weiss Financial. In return, Weiss would receive a sizable share of the proceeds for providing the service. And so, the deal with the devil was made. Over the years, the business relationship between the gangster and the pillar-of-the-community banker grew and prospered for both men.

Weiss' business connection with the Pirelli crew was handled as discreetly as possible. Multiple layers of complex corporate transactions were devised to cover the true nature of the relationship. Pirelli did not want to jeopardize Weiss' reputation as that of a hard-working, honest banker. Another benefit Perilli offered Weiss was to be a problem solver for the bank, if the need ever arose. Saul Workman was not the only problem Perilli's special skills solved for Benjamin Weiss. When a customer tried to avoid paying a loan back to Weiss Financial, Jimmy Perilli could be called upon to convince the bank's customer that non-payment was not an option. So, both of the old friends from the streets of the Lower East Side benefited by maintaining their bond of trust and a business relationship.

* * *

A week after the Senior Class prom in June 1988, David attended a two-week quarterback training academy hosted by the Chicago Bears in their training facility at the

University of Wisconsin in Platteville, Wisconsin. Jim McMahon, the starting quarterback for the 1986 Super Bowl champion Bears, along with a few of the coaches and team members, ran the camp. McMahon was the lead instructor for the young, aspiring quarterbacks. The four and five-star players came from all over the country to learn from McMahon and his championship teammates.

David was excited when he saw Mike Ditka, the head football coach of the Bears, walk out on the field to watch an afternoon of drills. Ditka took David aside for a private talk and told him that, if he continued to improve, he had what it takes to play in the National Football League.

Benjamin Weiss drove up to Platteville for the last day of the academy to gauge his son's progress and then drive David home. This gave the proud father an opportunity to chat with a couple professional football scouts, who were invited to the camp to talk to the boys about the business side of professional sports. The Bears chief scout told Benjamin that, if David fulfilled his potential in college, he would be a first-round draft-pick.

As soon as David returned home from the Bears' training academy, he had to pack for Bloomington, Indiana, to attend summer school at IU. David enrolled in summer school to be on campus, so he could use the weight training facilities to improve his muscular development and work with a sports dietician to improve his energy and strength. He ran at least five miles a day to increase his aerobic conditioning. He was determined to be in superb shape for the upcoming football season.

Media day was a real ego boost for the freshmen, as

well as the veteran players, who were the anticipated stars of the team. Sports reporters from the local television stations, area newspapers, and even a young writer for Sports Illustrated Magazine, attended to interview David and the other premier Hoosier football players. At a press conference in the Sports Media Center on the IU campus, Coach Mallory discussed his expectations for the 1988 team. Mallory told the reporters that he anticipated the team would be playing in a bowl game that year.

* * *

The night David got home from the quarterback training academy in Platteville, Wisconsin, Angelina came over to see him. She told him that she had a surprise announcement to make before he left for summer school. She was pregnant. David was absolutely beside himself with joy. After much hugging and kissing, the couple talked about planning a wedding. They agreed that it should be a small, private wedding in July, and only family and their closest friends would be invited.

Benjamin and Miriam took charge of the wedding arrangements with Angelina's help. Despite the couple's desire for a "small" affair, by including all members of the extended Weiss and the Mangano families, certain friends the parents insisted be invited, and the bride and groom's closest friends, there were over one hundred invited guests. Weisses in New York City were invited as were Manganos living in Syracuse, New York, along with the immediate families and Grassville friends. Benjamin hired an expensive wedding planner from Indianapolis, who planned a tasteful, and very expensive wedding celebration for the couple. David and Angelina decided to postpone their honeymoon until the Christmas holidays, so it wouldn't interrupt classes their first semester at IU. Benjamin arranged five nights at a beautiful resort on St. John's in the U.S. Virgin Islands.

David and Angelina were married on Saturday, July 23, 1988. Howard White was David's best man and Angelina's older sister, Teresa, was her maid of honor. The wedding took place at the Weiss' palatial mansion, next to the Olympic-size swimming pool. Angelina's parish priest officiated at the ceremony. A large tent was erected outside on the freshly trimmed lawn. The tent was filled with tables and chairs. The tent, tables, and the grounds were immaculately decorated with flowers and large plants. The planner arranged for a gigantic, multi-level wedding cake and ice statues filled with lobster and shrimp. There were various vegetable and fruit trays, cheese and cracker assortments, and many homemade Italian favorites, prepared from Angelina's mother's kitchen. The main course consisted of a 12-ounce bone-in filet mignon, gourmet garlic scalloped potatoes, roasted asparagus, and a dinner roll. A full-service bar was set up on the back patio of the mansion. Following the meal, a live band from Chicago Benjamin hired played fast and slow dance music for the guests until midnight.

Angelina's wedding dress was purchased from an exclusive dress shop on Michigan Avenue in downtown Chicago. Angelina selected the dress of her dreams for the wedding. Benjamin Weiss and the Manganos, who were multi-millionaires in their own right, decided that no expense would be spared on the wedding and reception. Miriam figured the wedding cost including the dress amounted to at least one hundred fifty-thousand dollars.

* * *

By the time regular football practice began in August, David was ready to fight for the starting QB position. His physical strength had increased. The high protein diet he'd followed in the summer added ten more pounds of muscle. His passing skills were even sharper. He'd memorized the entire play book, and he had the confidence to call audibles on the field when he saw a weakness in the defense to exploit. Still, during the first full-pad scrimmage David quickly discovered the difference between playing on a championship high school team and competing on a Division One, Big Ten team. College players were smarter, faster, more agile, and hit much harder than in high school.

In the team meeting prior to the opening game against Rice University, Coach Mallory informed the team that Dave Schnell, who was a junior, would be the starting quarterback. David Weiss would be second on the depth chart as the backup quarterback. David was disappointed that he didn't win the starting position, but he accepted the coach's decision with grace and looked forward to opportunities to prove he could contribute to the team on the second string. As the season progressed, David did earn some playing time and gained valuable experience, he hoped, for next year.

* * *

After the wedding, David and Angelina purchased a comfortable, 3-bedroom ranch house in Bloomington on W. Jordan Ave. next to a city park. Benjamin Weiss and Salvador Mangano split the cost of the home as a joint wedding gift to their children. Angelina completed her first semester in college, and then took the second semester off awaiting the anticipated birth of her baby.

After David and Angelina returned from their honeymoon trip the first week of Christmas break, all the members of the secret pact assembled at David and Angelina's new home in Bloomington. The get together was a shower/wedding/first-home party with the couple's closest friends. The party had a festive atmosphere with toasts and good-wishes by their friends for the happy, young couple. Angelina and David felt blessed to host their old friends in their new home. They held hands when describing the plans, they were making for their baby.

Eventually the conversation turned serious when the topic of the deceased Dalton boy came up. But everyone reconfirmed their commitment to keeping the "pact" a lifetime secret. The mood lightened again when the group moved out onto the patio to enjoy hamburgers and brats David cooked on a charcoal-fired grill. Stories about their first-semester college experiences were shared. There was much jovial laughter, along with cold beers and wine, as the long-time friends caught up on each other's' lives.

David's best friend, Howard White, told the group he was attending Harvard University in Cambridge, Massachusetts, and had definitely decided to major in political science. He hoped he would get admitted to Harvard Law School after completing his undergraduate studies. Staci Lykaios and Howard were still together as a couple, but they both admitted it was hard maintaining a long-distance relationship. Staci was attending Husson College in Bangor, Maine, studying restaurant management. Attending Husson was a compromise she'd made with her parents. Her parents wanted her to join the family restaurant business right after high school graduation, but Staci insisted that she wanted to go to college. So, the agreement was that she could attend college, so long as her education was geared toward management training. Husson offered Staci 90% tuition assistance, which delighted her parents. So, off she went to Bangor, Maine.

Steven Mills and Ann Gottlieb sat together most of the evening as the third of the three couples. However, they split up at the end of the summer before leaving Grassville for college. They were still friendly, but Ann was no longer in love with Steven. Steven still maintained a huge crush on Ann and held out hope that she might come back to him in the future. But Ann had no such intention. She had begun dating other guys and hoped to find Mr. Right at the University of Notre Dame in South Bend, Indiana. Ann planned to major in education. She definitely wanted to become a school teacher, but she also wanted to marry someone more interesting and with better prospects than good old boring, Steven Mills. Steven, as planned, went to Ball State University in Muncie, Indiana, to study business.

When the evening ended, the group said their good-byes and left to resume their own individual lives. Before departing, they all promised to see each other again within the year.

* * *

On March 10, 1989, a beautiful dark-haired baby boy entered the world and made his presence known with a loud and healthy wail. David and Angelina smiled with pride as they held Frank Mangano Weiss in their private room in the maternity ward of Indiana University Hospital. The baby was chunky, fat-checked with a pale complexion. In short, Frank Mangano Weiss was a very healthy little guy. David had wrung his hands in fear when Angelina went into labor. He couldn't help but worry about her survival of the ordeal, knowing that his own mother died during childbirth.

Chapter 14

Dave Schnell, a graduate of Elkhart (IN) Central High School, beat out David Weiss to retain his position as the starting quarterback for IU during the 1988 football season. Since Schnell led the Hoosiers to victories over both Michigan and Ohio State the previous year, David had been rather foolish to think he had much of a chance to beat out Schnell for the starting position. Sports Illustrated named Schnell the top high school football player in the country his senior year at Elkhart Central. The football world was shocked when Schnell turned down offers from Bear Bryant to play for Alabama's Crimson Tide and Joe Paterno to play at Penn State, and instead, decided to play for IU. With Schnell as the starter, and the highly touted freshman, David Weiss, as his backup, IU games were regularly attended by NFL scouts during the 1988 season.

In the 1989 season, David's sophomore and Schnell's senior year, David backed up Schnell as IU's QB once again. Dave Schnell was drafted by the Buffalo Bills following his graduation from IU. David Weiss dreamed about graduating and being drafted into the NFL too; although, he hoped to be drafted by the Chicago Bears, instead of the Buffalo Bills. David had not forgotten the compliments showered on him by Coach Mike Ditka during the Quarterbacks Academy he attended the summer after high school graduation.

David Weiss did become the Hoosiers' starting QB his junior and senior years. He played well his first year at the helm during the 1990 season, and he was off to an even better start his senior year. Many NFL scouts were drooling over the prospect of picking up David Weiss in the 1992 NFL draft. The team posted what would be a mediocre record of 7-4-1 for a powerhouse football program, like Michigan or Ohio State. But for Indiana, 1991 was another successful season led by another outstanding quarterback.

But David's sky-high dreams of playing for the Bears came crashing to earth near the end of the season during the Ohio State game on November 16, 1991. David was knocked out after being sacked while attempting a pass early in the fourth quarter. A six-foot four-inch 290-pound defensive lineman tore through IU's offensive line unblocked. He drove his helmet into David's side just as the IU QB turned to fake a handoff to his tailback. David didn't know what hit him as he was smashed onto the turf. He was carried off the field unconscious. In addition to a concussion, David sustained a season-ending injury to his right leg. He suffered a compound fracture of the femur and a blown-out knee. The final score of David's final college football game was Ohio State 20, Indiana 16. But even more disappointing to David than the loss to the arch-rival Buckeyes was the possibility that a pro career was in jeopardy due to the severity of his injuries. His fear turned out to be justified.

After multiple surgeries, including temporary pins in his upper leg and a cast to ensure proper mending of the bone, an ACL replacement, and repair of the medial meniscus, David began six months of physical therapy and rehab of his leg. At first, David was determined to completely recover and play football again. But at the end of the six-month rehab, a renowned orthopedic-specialist in Indianapolis, gave David the bad news. Dr. Schtellenboch agreed that the injured leg was healed to the extent that David was ambulatory again, but he advised that the structural integrity of the leg could never sustain what was required of a high school football player, let alone playing in the NFL. The doctor told David he would have to accept the fact that he could never play football again.

Both David and his father were crushed to hear Dr. Schtellenboch's opinion, but deep down neither of them were surprised. After the injury, David's stock had dropped dramatically as a pro prospect. He was drafted in the third round by the Cleveland Browns. But signing a contract would be conditioned on a medical release to play, and no legitimate doctor would give David a release. So, David and Benjamin had to accept that plans for David's future would have to be altered.

Benjamin Weiss had intended to keep David out of the day-to-day operations of Weiss Financial for at least five years after David's college graduation, or his pro-football career ended, whichever came first. Well, that time line had to change, since there would be no pro football, not even a rookie year. On the upside, David had a financial degree from one of the finest business schools in the country, and

David had expressed a sincere desire to ultimately join the family business since childhood.

Still, Benjamin Weiss did not want his son to join the business quite yet. The timetable for David to be appointed to a senior management position needed to be delayed awhile. Benjamin was worried that David was too young and idealistic to be able to handle learning about the bank's involvement with the mob. Benjamin feared that David's opinion of him would dramatically change once he found out his father was a banker for the Chicago mafia. Benjamin Weiss cherished the idealized father/son relationship he had with David. He dreaded alienating his only son in the waning years of his life. After all, Weiss was sixty-three years old and no longer a spring chicken. But, since time was no longer on his side, how could he bring David into the business without losing David's trust and admiration?

Weiss decided to have his trusted advisor and COO, Robert Levitt, help him develop a plan for bringing his son into the business. Surely, together they could find a position for David with the company, but that would not involve him in the less savory operations of Weiss Financial Group. Weiss wanted David to become the Chairman of the Board, upon his death. *By then, maybe Levitt and I will have figured out a way to amicably end the illegal activities with Jimmy Perilli. We just need a plan to disentangle Weiss Financial from the mob while David works his way up to being able to take over the company. If everything works out, David might not ever know of the illegal arrangement with the Perilli brothers.*

* * *

Benjamin Weiss invited his son to come home to Grassville from Bloomington for a weekend. He wanted to have a father/son talk about David's future career with Weiss Financial Group. Prior to their sit-down meeting, David and his dad played a round of golf at the Grassville Woods Country Club. After changing into slacks and sport coats, the Weiss men drove to the Villa Capri restaurant, which was owned by Staci Lykaios' parents. Father and son each ordered filet mignon and lobster for dinner.

After they were seated, Staci's father paid his respects at their table and informed them that Staci had graduated from Husson College with a degree in Restaurant Management. She had recently moved to Massachusetts to reside with her long-time boyfriend, Howard White.

Mr. Lykaios went on to say that Staci and Howard were trying to plan a future together, including marriage, but Howard wanted to wait until after he graduated from Harvard Law School to get married. Staci did not want to wait. Mr. Lykaios admitted ruefully that his daughter did not want to return to Indiana and manage her parents' restaurants. He said he knew that, as a dutiful daughter she felt obligated to help them out. After all, they paid for part of her education and they did have plans to turn over the restaurants to Staci in several years. "But," he sighed, "Staci never wanted to own the restaurants. She says she is only willing to help us on a limited basis. Staci wants us to sell the business when we're ready to retire. She's willing to return to help manage the restaurants until they were sold, but that's it," Mr. Lykaios concluded with a dismal look on his face.

David replied that he knew Staci loved her parents, and he was sure she would do everything she could to help them make a smooth transition into retirement. He didn't say that he also knew she envied him and Angelina for being married and having a child. He knew Staci had always wanted to marry Howard, settle down, and have a baby. And he knew she dreaded returning to Grassville even temporarily.

Just as the Weisses finished dessert, with perfect timing Robert Levitt appeared. He greeted David, and then took a seat at the hard wood table in one of the leather-upholstered chairs between Benjamin and his son. He explained that Mr. Weiss had requested his presence at the meeting. As it turned out, Levitt did most of the talking. He rhapsodized about how pleased he and Benjamin were that David had graduated at the top of his class with a degree in finance from Kelley School of Business. Levitt's voice dropped when he explained that, despite David's academic and athletic accomplishments it would be inappropriate to bring him into a senior management position at Weiss Financial without first giving him some practical experience and training in banking. "You will be more respected and better able to help run your father's banks and investment properties after you have earned your spurs, so to speak. We think beginning your career in finance at another banking institution will better prepare you for the important responsibility you will eventually have with the family business. Does that make sense to you, David?"

David respected and liked Robert Levitt, but he wondered why his father did not talk directly to him about this very important topic, *My future!* Surely Dad knows I would do whatever he asked, David thought. *So why did he bring in Levitt to engage in a conversation that ought to be father to son?* David loved and highly respected his dad, and was feeling confused and slightly hurt that Levitt was functioning more like a father than an employee or advisor for the Weiss family business. David guessed that his dad feared he would react negatively to the plan that he should be trained elsewhere before joining the Weiss corporation. David was sure his father wished only for his happiness. *But he evidently believes I'm not quite ready to join the management team of Weiss Financial. Alright, I get it. No big deal. It's just another hurdle to jump over before I can take my rightful place at Dad's elbow and help him run the company.*

David sat quietly for a moment to make sure his response was expressed in the right tone and came off sounding both mature and respectful. He finally said, "I understand what you want me to do and I will give your plan a try. I know you have my best interest at heart." David turned and looked directly into his father's eyes. "But Dad, I will admit to being disappointed with your plan. I had expected to be told at this meeting about an immediate opportunity for me at Weiss Financial. Nevertheless, I recognize you are better positioned to determine the best course for me at this initial stage of my career." David folded his hands and looked down.

Levitt looked at Weiss for a signal to respond. Instead, Benjamin spoke up, "Son, I realize you thought that once you finished college, you'd be playing football in the pros for at least a few years. When you retired from football, you'd be asked to join the senior management team of my business. But now playing pro football is out of the question, and you're being told that you will not be immediately joining our senior executive team. That's a double dose of disappointments you were not expecting. If you feel like I have misled you to some degree, please know that was not my intention. We should have had this conversation before you started college. For that I am very sorry. I think we were both so sure you'd be playing pro football; a backup plan was not discussed as it should have been." Benjamin reached over and squeezed his son's hands with both of his before continuing. "I understand you are feeling disappointed right now, but believe me, what we're suggesting as your entrée into the banking business will, as Robert expressed it, help you earn your spurs and the respect of others in the business. You will lead the company when you are ready. But, in our opinion, you are not quite ready, not just yet. By proving yourself at another financial institution first, you will be completely ready and able to better serve and lead Weiss Financial Group when it is your time."

David was surprised to feel a tear start to form at the corner of his eye, and quickly rubbed his eyes to avoid any unmanly show of emotion. His voice was controlled, when he replied, "Well Dad, I think you know I always planned to come back to Grassville, build a home, work with you at Weiss, and enjoy my family. However, I think I understand your reasoning for wanting me to prove myself at another company." David forced a smile across his broad face and said, "Dad, if you think it's best for the company and for the next generation of Weisses to put my dream of working at your side off for a while ok, I'll do it. I trust your judgment." He set his jaw with determination and asked, "So, what's next for me?"

Benjamin Weiss smiled with relief, slapped the table, and said, "Good! I've already spoken with my cousin, Walter Kohen in New York City. He will be delighted to offer you a middle management position for starters. Walter will teach you what you need to learn and then send you back to us. No doubt, Walter will end up wanting you to stay with him, after he's seen what you're capable of. So, don't get seduced by the temptations of New York! Don't forget, this is only a temporary situation. Once your training is completed in New York City and you're ready, I will bring you back and put you in charge of the management of my most valuable investment properties. After you've learned how to manage those properties, then you'll be ready to join Robert and me on our senior executive team. When I decide to retire, the entire company will be turned over to you to run, with, of course, Robert's assistance. And upon my death, you will be the sole owner of Weiss Financial Group." Benjamin leaned back in the well-padded chair with a look of supreme satisfaction twinkling in his eyes.

David felt his pulse quicken when his father mentioned his death. "But Dad!" he burst out, "You'll be around for a long-time. I want you to enjoy your grandchildren. Angelina and I plan to have a lot of kids and we appreciate everything you are doing to help us." Now, he took his dad's hands in his, squeezed them and smiled brightly back at his father.

"Thank you, Son. I'm very happy you accept our plan for your future and trust in my judgment." Benjamin had feared David might react angrily or been crushed with disappointment. Instead, his son had taken this disappointment like a man. And he clearly had complete faith in his father to continue to direct his future.

"No problem, Dad. Will I be paid a salary by Cousin Kohen, and will he provide employment benefits? Or will you be paying for my expenses, while I'm in New York being trained?"

"Hah! That's my boy!" Benjamin nearly shouted with glee and clapped his son on the shoulder. "See Robert, he's already thinking like a businessman." Levitt chuckled politely, as the senior Weiss went on. "David, you will be a regular employee of Parkview Bank. I'm sure my cousin, Walter Kohen will treat you well, but, if there are expenses you need help with that your salary doesn't cover, you can be sure that I will always step in to take care of your family." He winked at David and Levitt nodded knowingly. Benjamin continued, "There are plenty of nice places to rent in NYC. I think you and Angelina will really like living in downtown Manhattan. But don't forget, I want you to return to Grassville and me, when it is time to come back home. And Son, don't forget, Grassville will always be home for you."

"Don't worry, Dad. I will come back to Grassville when you decide I'm ready."

When the three men stood up to leave the restaurant,

David and his father embraced. Benjamin told David to go on out to the car, "I just need a minute more of Robert's time." The two older men watched David limp toward the exit. Then, Weiss thanked Levitt for helping to make the meeting go smoothly. The two of them had carefully planned the day to gently guide David toward their desired end. The golf outing, dinner, Levitt's timely appearance, it had all been strategically planned to manipulate David to accept the decisions they'd made for him. Once again, Weiss was grateful for how deftly Levitt had played his part. *Levitt is worth every penny I pay him.* It was critical that David accept the plans they'd made for him while preserving his trust in both of them. Otherwise, Weiss' ultimate plans for the family fortunes might not unfold as he wanted.

Robert Levitt also felt relieved that the first step in the plan for David succeeded. He had seen a side of David that Benjamin seemed to refuse to recognize. But thankfully, once again David did not lose control of his temper in front of his father. Yet, Levitt realized that Weiss must be aware on some level of David's potential for blowing up. Why else was he so concerned about his son's reaction to their recommendations for his future?

Chapter 15

When George Nelson turned twenty-one, he began to work a forty-hour work week at Moretti's liquor store. He enrolled in a course to become an over-the-road truck driver. The course included book work and hands-on learning to drive a semi-truck and tractor. The course was expensive and used most of the money George was able to save from his paycheck and selling pot for Stenzi, but he was sure it would be worth the investment in the long run. Some companies needed drivers so badly they paid the course fee, if a driver agreed to work for them following graduation. Unfortunately, George didn't have any connections in the trucking industry when he enrolled in the driver's course, so he had to pay his own tuition. But following graduation, George was immediately offered a job driving a semi-truck for Central Indiana Transport, a private carrier that hauled auto parts from Indianapolis to Michigan, Illinois, and Ohio. His route gave him ample time to return to Indianapolis the same day, but with a different load for the return trip. The pay and benefits were far better than what he had been earning at the liquor store and working for Stenzi combined. George had recently turned twenty-one, when he enrolled in the course and was one of the youngest drivers to graduate and get a job.

George gave notice to Moretti two-weeks before he was to start work for Central Indiana Transport, but decided he'd continue to work for Stenzi on the side. George made enough money driving for Central Indiana Transport, he put a down-payment on a used pickup truck. He could now afford to move to a nicer apartment, but he didn't. Although he hadn't stuck strictly to his four-point plan, George was determined to create a life for himself better than his father's. He saved money to invest in something substantial. His future! His life was moving in the right direction. For the first time in his life, George felt truly happy. He had cleaned up; he no longer looked like a Hoosier hick. The union contract that covered drivers at Central Indiana Transport allowed George to see a dentist on a regular basis and get a yearly physical exam. George's health improved. He changed his diet, and he started working out at a local gym. He continued shopping at Goodwill to save money, but the clothes George bought came from high-end donors to Goodwill, so even his wardrobe improved. Slowly but surely, George Nelson was becoming a different man than the one that ran away from Grassville. George Nelson had learned the lesson that success would come from hard work, saving money, and always trying to improve himself.

Chapter 16

David, Angelina, and baby Frank arrived in New York City an hour and a half late. The plane was delayed in Chicago for a minor repair. It was a sparkling, sunny day when their flight finally landed at LaGuardia Airport around two in the afternoon. Except for the delay, the non-stop flight from O'Hare International to LaGuardia was uneventful. The Weiss family checked into the Marriott, a luxury hotel, on Broadway in downtown Manhattan. A bell hop directed the family to the two-room suite arranged for their stay by Benjamin Weiss. The hotel's management agreed to provide the suite for the Weisses, until they found a suitable apartment to rent.

The following day, David met with a real estate agent from Pickering & Son to begin hunting for an apartment. He told Mikael Sandel, the apartment-rental expert for Pickering, "I want a nice place, with a good view, clean, furnished, two or three bedrooms, near Central Park."

Sandel flipped the bangs of his bleached-blond hair and cocked his head before replying, "Is there a price range to consider, Mr. Weiss? Or is that not a consideration?"

"What would you say it would cost to move into a place like I described?"

"Well, that depends on the property, what floor you pick, the amenities, and the condition of the apartment," Sandel said as he stroked his dyed-blond goatee thoughtfully. He gazed back at David expectantly.

"I think I would have a better idea if we take a look at a few places resembling what I've described. But you need to know, Mr. Sandel, I'm on a very tight schedule. So, could we start looking as soon as this afternoon? What do you think?"

"I totally understand, Mr. Weiss," Sandel whipped his pocket scheduler out of the soft-leather, sling bag hanging on his right shoulder. He quickly scanned the calendar mumbling to himself. He gave David a bright smile and said, "Uh yes, I can make this afternoon work. I've got several properties in mind that I think you might like. We're not far from one of them, but I'll have to give the listing agent a call and see if we can visit today. How does that sound?" Mikael stole an admiring look at David's perfectly shaped physique, while he conferred with Angelina.

His wife nodded her assent, so David turned back to the realtor and brusquely explained, "We're in a hurry to leave our hotel suite, so, go ahead and give the agent a call. I'm highly motivated, and so is my wife, to move into an upscale apartment and get established somewhere in the Manhattan area. I'm starting a new position at the Parkview Bank."

Out of the corner of his eye, David had seen Sandel admiring his form. He chuckled to himself and thought, *I'm not in Grassville anymore, am I?* David had encountered all kinds of characters at IU Bloomington that he didn't even imagine existed while he was growing up in rural Grassville. His college experience broadened his experience and David now thought himself to be quite liberal-minded. So, he didn't feel offended by Sandel's obvious sexual interest in him. David's reaction beyond amusement was just mild curiosity as to whether Mikael was homosexual or bi-sexual. David knew he had nothing to fear; Sandel would surely do nothing to jeopardize a relationship with clients like the Weisses through whom the realtor would receive a premium commission for his services. David did notice with admiration and curiosity the large ring on Mikael's right index finger. It looked to be solid gold with a large diamond placed in the center of the ring. No doubt, it was made especially for the wearer. *Hmm, a family heirloom or a gift from a former lover?*

While the search got underway that afternoon, it was unsuccessful through three days of multiple showings. But finally, Mikael found the almost-perfect apartment for the Weisses. It was in an elegant building close to Parkview Bank, David's place of employment. The apartment was on the tenth floor. It was nicely furnished with a spectacular view of the city, although not Central Park. It had two bedrooms, one a master bedroom suite, a full bath, and a half bath. The apartment was recently redecorated. When they entered, Angelina immediately noticed and appreciated a fresh and clean aroma within the apartment. Mikael explained that David and Angelina would be the first occupants since the renovation was completed. Angelina was especially delighted with the upscale ambience. She was excited by the prospect of living in Manhattan and being the wife of an up and coming banker. "What an ideal place to introduce baby Frank to the world!" she exclaimed.

The following Monday morning, David met with his second cousin, Walter Kohen, to discuss what his training would entail. He was assigned to begin working in the business and individual loan office of the main branch of Parkview Bank. Kohen broke an unwritten rule when he located his small-sized community bank in the heart of Manhattan. Most Manhattan banks are large and influential institutions with thousands of locations throughout the nation. But Kohen found a niche with some of the less affluent members of the Manhattan community. Kohen's bank was well positioned to serve their needs. His customers valued personal service and the lack of needless, red-tape requirements of the larger banking corporations. It was basically the same concept that the elder Weiss successfully used when he established Weiss Financial in Indiana.

As agreed, David's progress at the bank was being monitored by Robert Levitt for Weiss Financial Group. Benjamin Weiss was pleased with his son's progress as was his cousin, Walter Kohen. Kohen informed Benjamin, in one of their otherwise mundane, business conversations, that in the event Weiss Financial didn't want or need David to return to Indiana, Kohen would be happy to keep him at Parkview Bank. Weiss thanked him for complimenting his son, but reminded Kohen that David was there for training and to learn the business. Benjamin made it very clear to everyone that he wanted his son to eventually join him in running his Indiana banks. Kohen understood, but figured there was no harm in trying to recruit David Weiss for his company long term. After all, Kohen and Weiss were part of the same German family that originated in Munich and immigrated to the USA a generation ago. Since it would still be working with family, maybe David would decide he loved New York and would like to stay. Shouldn't that be David's decision Walter mused, but didn't make that point with Cousin Benjamin.

As the months past, David learned the principles of running a successful community bank. The lessons he learned in the Kelley financial business courses he took at Indiana University made a lot more sense to him. It was gratifying to compare his actual, day-to-day experience with the textbook theories, and to see how the theories worked in practice. David was genuinely happy working at Parkview Bank. He knew it was a way station on the path his father planned for him. He had initially resented his father's plan and didn't see the value in working in New York and being trained by his dad's cousin. But David had come to appreciate the wisdom behind the plan, which was apparently co-created by his father and Robert Levitt. David never questioned the managerial brilliance of his dad, or Robert Levitt. He mainly resented the way it was presented. Having Levitt introduce the plan for his future, well, it made David feel like a commodity, rather than his father's only son. But he was long over that. He'd developed a much better understanding of how family and business mixed working with Cousin Walter. There was family, and there was business, and you had to recognize where the line was drawn. He knew his father trusted Robert Levitt with the most intimate details of the business. Levitt was after all the Weiss Financial advisor and COO. So why shouldn't he be trusted to participate in planning the future of the heir-apparent to the business?

* * *

During the first two years at Parkview Bank, David received practical training and experience in running all the departments in the bank. When his third year in NYC commenced, unbeknownst to David, discussions were occurring back in Grassville about bringing him home.

Robert Levitt and Benjamin Weiss met in Weiss' office to begin planning the next phase of David Weiss' career. Levitt told Weiss that he thought, given David's progress, that it was about time to put David in charge of the company's real estate investments, in accordance with the plan they devise more than twenty-four months ago. However, Levitt's opinion that the transition should occur fairly soon was not well received by Weiss. Weiss reminded Levitt that he did not want his son to learn about the Perilli brothers and their involvement with Weiss Financial.

"I am well aware of your concern, Benjamin," Levitt replied. "But you know as well as I do that David will eventually learn of the Perillis' reliance on Weiss Financial to launder illegal money. Having David in charge of the real estate investments will not open that door. As long as we keep the real estate investment properties separate from the banking operation, we can keep David in the dark about the Perillis."

Benjamin agreed Levitt's plan would maintain a wall between the illegal operations of the bank and his son's role in the business, but he dearly wanted to disentangle the business from the mob. If David someday learned of the dirty-money operation, but it was over, hopefully, he would forgive his father. Benjamin slapped his hand on the desktop and declared that they would have to make a trip to Chicago and meet with the Perillis to discuss terminating their money laundering operation. Levitt called Perilli and set up a Monday afternoon meeting at 2:30 p.m. in the Coq d'Or cocktail lounge in the Drake Hotel on Michigan Avenue. The men had met at the Coq d'Or before and felt comfortable there, because, as Perilli said, "It's staffed by people we know, and it's a secure place to discuss business before the after-work crowd arrives." Levitt asked Pirelli to reserve a booth in the far, back corner for added privacy.

When Weiss and Levitt walked through the lobby of the Drake Hotel, they paid no attention to the lush carpet and magnificent chandelier. Their minds were fixed on the difficult discussion they anticipated with Jimmy Perilli in the Coq d'Or. The cocktail lounge was appointed with blends of rich, wood paneling, rogue-leather accents, and a cozy glow from dim lighting intended to evoke a nostalgic vibe, described by its marketing literature as "a gentlemen's drinking room of the early 1800's."

Perilli arrived first and was smoking a big Cuban cigar and drinking a glass filled with Sambuca, when Weiss and Levitt arrived. "Welcome to the Windy City, my friends," Perilli said in Italian as he rose and grasped each of the men's hands in his big paws.

Weiss responded, "Grazie, Prego." Then he switched to English. "I've lost most of my Italian, since living in Indiana, Jimmy. It used to be helpful to be bilingual in our business, but those days have long passed, I'm afraid. Let's speak English, shall we?"

"Sure, no problem. But it is important to remember the past and how our relationship was formed. I can still see you as a small, tough, Jewish kid, who beat up much bigger kids. And, you had a razor-sharp mind. Everybody in the neighborhood was impressed with you then, and look at you now – a great man with a great business. It makes me happy to know our business is part of the reason you've become so successful. Yes, it's clearly remarkable. You are a very lucky and gifted man, Benjamin Weiss." Perilli ended his litany of compliments with a sly grin on his face.

Weiss knew what Perilli was up to, bringing up their shared past. Jimmy Perilli was nick-named "The Fist", because his punches were so powerful. But he wasn't just a big palooka. He was clever too. Reminiscing about the past and showering Weiss with compliments was Perilli's strategy to remind Weiss that their long-time relationship was a key aspect of Weiss' own success. Dissolving the relationship would have consequences; no matter the reason.

Benjamin made the case to his old friend that there were, no doubt, things in Perilli's life he did not want revealed to his son and daughter. So, surely Jimmy could understand why he wanted to shield David from the less savory aspects of their business. The Fist nodded sympathetically, but pointed out that Weiss knew this would happen someday, if he brought his son into the business. "Benjamin, it is up to you how you separate family from business. We are friends, but our relationship is based strictly on business. If our organization can no longer use your bank, all of us would suffer. My friend," Pirelli continued in a sympathetic but firm tone, "If our special arrangement is messed with, well, Bruno Altobello is a father too and fair-minded. But as the Boss of the Altobello crime family he will always put business first. How could I justify the difficulties that will arise, if our business is so disrupted that payments were short or missed. There would be very grave consequences, my old friend."

The fearful and respectful tone in Perilli's voice was evident, as he talked about Altobello, the man who the mobsters called "Il Duce" (the leader). It became obvious to Weiss and Levitt that Perilli would never cross his Il Duce. Altobello's temper, when he felt betrayed, was legendary. Rumors had it that, instead of hiring someone to do the job, on several occasions he pulled out his own pistol and shot a lieutenant in the head during a "business meeting", because the subordinate dared to disagree with Il Duce. Men who worked for Altobello whispered that he was like a time bomb ready to explode whenever he perceived that his authority was threatened. Weiss respected Altobello's accomplishments, but secretly thought that, if the rumors were true, Il Duce's intelligence and judgment were questionable. Weiss believed that it could be useful to be feared rather than loved in Altobello's position. But acting like a wild animal went too far. Weiss thought that a key to success, whether as a mobster or a private businessman, was maintaining strict control over one's temper and exercising good judgment. Weiss' relationship with Perilli was profitable and it gave him the ability to handle difficult situations, if the need arose, without getting his hands dirty. He and Perilli had worked well together over several decades, and he was well aware of the advantages gained and that there would be risks, if he decided to rock the boat.

When it looked like they'd reached an impasse, Levitt finally spoke up. He conceded that simply terminating the relationship was too dangerous for all concerned. He proposed that he and Weiss look for another solution to the problem. "Between the two of us, I'm sure we can come up with something acceptable," Levitt said spreading his hands. "I'm sure we can find a way to continue sheltering your activities without having to end our long-time banking relationship."

Perilli was not completely mollified. He glanced nervously back and forth at the two men sitting across the table. And then looking intently at Weiss and said, "I'm relying on you to find that solution."

Weiss nodded in agreement, but a bead of sweat slowly ran down his right temple. He was clearly worried. *What if there was no solution?* Trusting business associates is one thing, but when they are mobsters, well, Weiss knew he would be on thin ice, if he put Pirelli in jeopardy with Il Duce. *But what if David discovered something amiss and without realizing the implications reported it to the authorities? The company could face an inquiry from the state banking commission.* Weiss felt like he was in a small boat with sharks on both sides.

When the subject was exhausted, Perilli declared the business meeting at an end. He invited his guests to exit the bar and join him in the Cape Cod Restaurant across the lobby of the Drake Hotel. He treated them to a fabulous seafood feast of lobster, shrimp, and Dover sole. At the conclusion of the meal, Weiss and Levitt shook hands with Perilli. During the drive back to Grassville Weiss and Levitt discussed different options to further insulate the bank from the Indiana state banking regulatory commission. But even if they successfully implemented a more stringent insulating strategy, at some point in time, Weiss had to assume his son would probably learn about the special arrangement with the Perillis. That was what Benjamin Weiss feared the most. He didn't want his son to know who he really was. No parent wants their children to see their dark side.

* * *

Several days later, Levitt called David in Manhattan and informed him it was time for him to come back to Grassville and join the company. When David told

Angelina the news, she was as ecstatic as he was. They'd enjoyed their time in NYC, but Grassville was home. And that's where they wanted to raise their growing family.

Angelina surprised and delighted David, when she revealed she was pregnant for the second time. The gynecologist used an ultra-sound machine to look at the baby's development and determined the couple would be having another boy. David was sure his father would be pleased that they planned to name their second son, Benjamin.

Chapter 17

Upon David and Angelina's return from Manhattan, the elder Weiss, now 65 years of age, hosted a family only, welcome home party for the young couple at his residence. The Manganos and Weisses enjoyed a sumptuous meal of an array of steaks, Italian specialties, salads, and desserts. It was a joyful day for the combined families. The highlight of the celebration for the elder members of the clans was playing with little Frankie. He was a cute and lively little boy. His Grassville kin were impressed with how much he'd grown.

Just before the guests tucked into the lavish meal, David and Angelina announced that they were expecting their second child, another baby boy. Benjamin joyfully offered a toast for a safe pregnancy and a healthy birth. After the toast, David surprised his dad by announcing that the child would be named Benjamin. Several tears were visible in the elder Weiss' eyes when Angelina and David referred to their unborn baby son as Benjamin, Jr.

After all the guests departed, Benjamin asked David to meet him in his study before going to bed. He said there was a matter of business to discuss. David was surprised his dad wanted to talk business late on a Sunday night right after the homecoming celebration. *What is so important it can't wait until tomorrow?* Before David entered his father's office, he poked his head through the door. Benjamin was sitting behind his desk with his head in his hands. David was alarmed, because his father looked more than just tired after a long day of playing host. The elder Weiss appeared to be uneasy and troubled. David cleared his throat as he quietly entered the room in stocking feet. "Uh, Dad, thank you for the wonderful home-coming celebration. It was certainly more than we expected." David eyed his father apprehensively.

Benjamin Weiss arose from his chair and embraced his son. "It has been over two years since you've been in my private office," Weiss said sadly. "Your presence has been missed by both Miriam and myself. There is something you need to know, and I wanted you to hear it directly from me." Weiss still gripped David's shoulders, but held him at arm's length for a moment longer. Then, he asked David to take a seat. "I know you love Miriam. She's been as much as a mother to you as your own mother would have been; God rest her soul." Benjamin sighed, then continued, "If I hadn't married your mother, Miriam could have been your birth mother. You see," Weiss said clearing his throat momentarily, "I was dating your mom and Miriam at the same time. I was allowed the luxury of deciding which woman I wanted to spend my life with. Both were wonderful, exciting, and beautiful ladies. They were, of course, different in several ways. I chose your mother over Miriam, but I was honest about my feelings to both of them, at the time."

David stared at his father dumbstruck and speechless for a moment. Finally, he said, "I had no idea, Dad!"

Weiss looked at his befuddled son. Benjamin reached out and patted David's knee sympathetically. "When your mother passed away, I turned to Miriam for help raising you. Frankly, raising a child as a single parent felt overwhelming at the time. I'm an entrepreneur and a businessman. I had expected your mother to be your primary caretaker, while I concentrated on making the family financially secure by building the business." He gave David a rueful smile. "I trusted Miriam to help raise you. The responsibilities of fatherhood were daunting, as I'm sure you now know." David returned his dad's smile. "But Son, I hope you know that you are more precious to me than anything else in the world." Tears formed in Benjamin's eyes as he continued, "Miriam graciously agreed to help me out. Over the years, she began to think of you as her child. We both love you very much. I want you to know that we are very proud of how well you've turned out. I've wanted to tell you the full story about my relationship with Miriam, but I was unsure of how you'd react. Now that you've matured and become a successful businessman, husband, and father, I am confident you will understand why I wanted you to know before anyone else - I've asked Miriam to become my wife." Weiss' eyes looked searchingly into David's. "And she has agreed to my proposal."

David's face lit up with a broad smile. "Oh my God, Dad! I had no idea growing up, about your true feelings for Miriam. But I used to day-dream that you two would get married! I always wished that Miriam would become more than my nanny and your employee. I did think of her as my real mother. Miriam is the only mother I've ever known." David enthused, "If you two get married, it would be a dream come true for me!" David jumped up and lovingly pulled his father up from his swivel chair and hugged him tightly. Now, it was his turn to hold his father at arm's length and look deeply into his eyes. "Dad, this is really incredible news, and I'm so happy for you, for Miriam, for all of us." He squeezed his father's shoulders warmly, and then chuckled. "But this is another example of a conversation we should have had years ago." David took his father's hand and shook it vigorously. "Congratulations Dad, I'm glad you can be truly happy once again."

When David finally released his father's hand, Benjamin indicated they should sit again and resumed a serious tone. "I want you to know that, after Miriam and I are married your position in the company will remain what we've always planned. Upon my death, ownership and control will be bequeathed to you. I want you to feel totally secure about that. I have made the financial arrangements so that Miriam will always be taken care of after I'm gone, assuming I predecease her. Levitt has taken care of those arrangements in my will and trust agreement. I'm not as young as I used to be, and I hate to admit it, but my health isn't as good as it could be. As you know, I've got a bad heart. I plan to retire within a few years. Miriam and I would like to have a few years to travel and relax after my retirement."

David cut in, "Dad, you've got plenty of good years ahead of you. Don't talk like you're in failing health and at death's door! You are going to have many years of happiness with Miriam by your side. I'm sure of it," David said with an even wider grin.

"Son, I'm very pleased you will be joining me, starting tomorrow morning, with management responsibilities in the Weiss Financial Group. As promised, you will be running our real estate investment-property division until I retire. Then, you will be made CEO of the entire company. I hope you know how happy I am to have you join the company business. And thank you, for honoring me by planning to name your second boy Benjamin." Both men smiled happily at each other. "As to running the business, there is one piece of advice I want to give you, and hope you will take it to heart." The smile faded from the elder Weiss' face and he gave David a penetrating look. "Never trust anyone completely that you make deals with. This even includes our company advisor and COO, Robert Levitt. He's a loyal, intelligent, hard-working, and dependable man, but that does not mean you should blindly accept all of his advice. While it is his job to look out for our best interests, it will be you who will bear the final responsibility for any decision made on behalf of the company. Robert's position does not give him the authority to make the final decision about anything. That responsibility is mine for now. Once I'm gone, that responsibility will be yours."

David embraced his father again and said, "Everything will work out fine, Dad. You'll see, I'm ready to start shouldering some of the burden. Please don't worry about me." As if on cue, Miriam entered the room. The two men stood and the three of them embraced in a group hug. With his hands still on their shoulders, David said, "I love you two very much and I'm happy you're going to be together."

Miriam smiled and responded, "Thank you, David." She pulled him to her and wrapped him in her loving arms. "I've dreamed about this moment since you were a young child. I'm so happy for you, Angelina, little Frank, your father, and for myself. Today, will be one of the most memorable and wonderful days of my life," Miriam started shaking with emotion as tears flowed down her cheeks.

* * *

Several months later, Benjamin Weiss announced he was going to New York City to attend a banking convention. He planned to spend some time with his Cousin Walter and to thank him for successfully preparing David for the coming challenges.

Miriam hugged Benjamin and kissed him on the cheek. She was happy he would be able to visit his family in New York. She was also pleased Benjamin's time away would free her up for a shopping spree in Chicago with her best friend, Sybil. They were going to find the perfect wedding dress for her upcoming Jewish nuptial ceremony. Miriam and Benjamin planned to have a traditional Kiddushin, Hebrew for a sanctification or dedication ceremony. What Miriam didn't know was that Benjamin planned to purchase an extravagant diamond engagement ring and wedding set for her, while he was in New York. Vanessa Goldberg's family owned a chain of exclusive jewelry stores in New York. Robert Levitt had already made arrangements and scheduled an appointment for his boss at the Goldberg's main store in downtown Manhattan.

The Secret Pact

Chapter 18

After arriving in New York City, Weiss took a taxi to downtown Manhattan to purchase the rings. As Weiss began to cross Park Avenue at the insertion of East 49th Street, in route to Goldberg's Uptown Jewelers, a dark van careened out of an alley. Weiss heard tires screeching as the van turned wildly onto Park Avenue heading right toward him. Weiss barely had time to make eye contact with a large Hispanic-looking man behind the wheel before the van slammed into him. Weiss' body went air borne and then crash-landed; his head smacked against the curb making a crunching sound as it hit.

When the EMT's arrived, they realized the victim of a hit-and-run had suffered a traumatic head injury and was probably bleeding internally. The injuries were severe and life-threatening. The unconscious man in a torn, conservatively-tailored suit was swiftly loaded into the ambulance. Benjamin Weiss died in the ambulance on the way to the Mount Sinai Hospital.

Witnesses to the accident described to the cops, who arrived on the scene simultaneous with the ambulance, that the van looked like it was out of control. One semihysterical elderly lady shouted, "He must have been drunk! You should have seen the way he came barreling out of the alley. He didn't stop or even look before he ran down that poor man!" The police put out a BOLO for the dark-brown van, described by witnesses. Unfortunately, no one could recall a license plate number. A grizzled old cop muttered to his rookie partner, "Poor sucker prob'ly never knew what hit him. And the bastard that did it was prob'ly so drunk he won't know he was in an accident, until he wakes up tomorrow and sees the damage to his van. If it's even his van."

The NYPD Homicide Department opened an investigation and assigned two detectives to track down the "large, Hispanic in appearance man" described by witnesses to the hit-and-run. After the victim's identity was established by multiple documents found on his person and in his wallet, an officer called the number indicated as Benjamin Weiss' home phone. Miriam passed out and fell to the floor while the officious voice on the phone explained that he needed to speak to Mr. Benjamin Weiss' next of kin due to his death.

After she recovered her senses, Miriam called the NYPD for the details of Benjamin's death. As soon as she was able to control the sobs that wracked her chest, she called David to deliver the news. He was devastated. Since he was an infant when his mother died, this was the first death of anyone close to him he had to deal with. It felt like all the air was sucked out of his lungs. He sunk to his knees crying inconsolably.

* * *

When Robert Levitt was notified about his boss' death, he made arrangements for Weiss' body to be returned to Grassville via private jet. No expenses were spared for Benjamin Weiss' funeral services, which were attended by all the prominent citizens of Grassville, Weiss business associates, banking clients, politicians, Weiss family members from New York, and, of course, the immediate Weiss family members.

Although Benjamin Weiss was Jewish, he hadn't been inside a synagogue for many years. David decided not to contact a Chevra Kadisha, a holy group of people who take charge of the funeral arrangements. Instead, he, Miriam, and Robert Levitt made all the arrangements for the service. It was an outdoor service at Benjamin's home, on the pool deck. At the Lavayah (Jewish grave-side ceremony), David sat with Angelina, little Frank, and Miriam on folding chairs at the gravesite in front of the casket. Following recital of traditional Jewish prayers in both Hebrew and English, cemetery workers lowered Weiss' casket into the ground. Family members helped cover the casket with shovels filled with dirt. When the casket was completely covered with dirt, the Rabbi said the final prayer, "May Hashem comfort you among the mourners of Zion and Jerusalem." Before the mourners, according to ancient Jewish custom, each one placed a small rock on Benjamin's gravesite. The custom originated to keep the body safe from predatory, corpse-eating animals.

After all the other attendees left, David and Miriam remained at the gravesite. They placed two dozen red roses on the ground at the gravesite. After she placed the last rose on the grave Miriam stood for a moment silently staring at the headstone with Benjamin Weiss' name engraved on it. Then she broke down and started bawling uncontrollably. David wrapped his arms around her and rocked slowly back and forth.

David drove Miriam back to the Weiss mansion. During the drive, Miriam continued sobbing. David heard her babbling that she "will ever remain Miriam Gleiser and will never be Miriam Weiss." David helped her to bed and made sure she took a sedative to quiet her nerves and help her sleep. For his part, David felt like he was living in a fog. He kept hearing over and over the voice of the New York detective saying his father was dead, apparently killed by a drunk driver. It still didn't seem real. *How could that bull of a man, his father, Benjamin Weiss be dead?*

As was his duty, Robert Levitt handled all the immediate matters required to keep Weiss Financial operating as smoothly as possible. He dared not speak it, but one of Levitt's first thoughts, when he learned of Weiss' untimely death, was to wonder whether the Perilli brothers were involved. He hoped not, because then, when David Weiss was installed as the CEO and owner, his life might be in danger too. Levitt well remembered Jimmy Perilli's comment that, despite their long association, the relationship was ultimately a business relationship, not family. Was that comment during the meeting at the Drake Hotel meant to remind them who their best customer really was and what the consequence of severing that relationship could be? Given that Perilli and his brother were ruthless criminals and killers, to them, "business" included wiping out anyone who opposed them. Levitt knew he was going to have to guide David very carefully to avoid Perilli's grasp. The more he pondered the question, the more Levitt doubted that Jimmy Perilli would have his long-time friend and associate killed. Benjamin had backed off trying to disentangling the bank from the Perillis' business. But Levitt was certainly not going to ask Jimmy Perilli whether he'd taken a hit out on Weiss. Robert Levitt had to accept that, if the Perillis did arrange Benjamin's death, no one would ever find out.

* * *

Eight days after his father was laid to rest, David finally felt up to dealing with business again. He called Levitt to discuss what steps needed to be taken. Levitt suggested the first step should be to review Benjamin's will and trust arrangements. David knew it was time to exert his well-honed personal discipline no matter how heavy the grief was that he still felt over the loss of his father. So, he replied, "I want to get this behind me as soon as possible. Meet me tomorrow morning in my father's office and we will begin transferring the stock. You can start turning over the operation slowly to me."

Levitt responded, "No problem. We can begin the process starting tomorrow morning, David, if that is your wish. Is eight a.m. too early?"

"Absolutely not. If you come around seven, I'll have Millie cook breakfast for the two of us."

Robert Levitt pulled into the Weiss' driveway the following morning exactly at seven a.m. He parked his Mercedes in front of the home and found David at the front door to greet him. They were served omelets, toast, juice, and coffee by Millie, the cook, in the screened in porch overlooking the pool. Before getting down to business, the two men quietly enjoyed the fruits of Millie's cooking and gazed out across the estate. The horse stables were visible off in the distance. Levitt delicately wiped his mouth with a napkin, cleared his throat, and said, "David, I first want to make sure we are clear on my own position within the company. It was your father's wish that I would continue as the family advisor and the COO. However, I don't want to be presumptuous. Whether I continue in that role is now your decision. With your father's passing, you are the CEO and sole owner of the Weiss Financial Group."

David remembered his father's advice about trust and that Levitt should remain the COO and family advisor, but that David should keep a watchful eye on him. David had decided that he would maintain the status quo and he assumed over time Levitt would earn his trust. If not, he'd get rid of him and pick someone else to help run the business. So, David assured Levitt that he wanted him to retain all the responsibilities he'd been given by Benjamin. With that matter behind them, Levitt updated his new boss on the financial condition of the company and described all plans Benjamin and he were working on for further development and expansion of the business.

David asked pertinent questions as Levitt talked him through the many details about the company's operation Levitt thought David needed to know. David said he thought it would be wise to postpone making important decisions affecting the company until after he completed a full review of the company's books and records, visited the branches, and checked on the real estate holdings. Both men were feeling pleased with how well their new relationship had begun. But then, Levitt told David he had a matter to discuss that David might find difficult to hear. Levitt hated to do it, but he knew it would make matters worse if he put it off.

Levitt grimaced and then launched into a description of the Perillis' and the bank's unique relationship. He carefully described all the services Weiss Financial provided to the Chicago mob through its many holding companies and disguised subsidiaries. And, he informed David that the Perillis' organization was the bank's largest customer.

At first, David couldn't believe what he was hearing coming out of Robert Levitt's mouth. He stopped the older man and asked whether the activities of the bank with the Perilli organization were illegal. Without hesitation, Levitt affirmed that, indeed, the bank was engaged in various illegal activities with the Perillis. He went on to explain the long history of Benjamin Weiss' relationship with Jimmy Perilli, and how his father and the gangster became life-long friends starting in the streets of New York City. "When Jimmy Perilli asked your father for a favor, how could he refuse his old friend? Jimmy told your dad it would just be a one-time deal, but it quickly expanded from there."

David was shocked and surprised as he listened to Robert Levitt describe the details of the bank's illegal service to help Perilli launder his gangland money. *How could my father have been so stupid and careless to risk losing everything he worked so hard for? Why would he risk going to prison?* David's initial reaction as to what he should do was, *I have to quickly oversee the expulsion of the Perillis from my bank.*

When David expressed that desire to Levitt, the elder man's reply was, "That's exactly what your father had been working on; a strategy to accomplish a termination of the relationship with the Perillis prior to his retirement and your ascension to CEO. Your dad was working on a plan and he was certain several changes could be made that would completely insulate the bank from any further illegalities." However, Levitt insisted that, "For the time being anyway, it would be in Weiss Financials best interest to preserve the Perilli business due to the size of their accounts." Levitt explained that the company risked its very viability, if David abruptly ended the relationship.

David scratched his head as he considered Levitt's advice. After collecting his thoughts, he asked Levitt to arrange a meeting with Jimmy Perilli as soon as possible. Before the meeting Levitt would need to explain all the changes that Benjamin had planned to pursue to limit the bank's exposure to further risk. David said he wanted the Perillis to understand that any changes his father had planned were not negotiable. But after he calmed down, he asked Levitt whether he thought Jimmy Perilli would understand and agree to the changes demanded. "After all, the current relationship is not sustainable and will eventually end badly for both parties. Even a gangster must understand that!"

David told Levitt that he learned a lot from Cousin Walter on how to deal with difficult people. Walter's advice was to always take charge first, which will give you an immediate advantage. Never act subservient to the opposing party, even if he was a mobster. Walter Kohen had told David stories of facing down crime bosses in New York City. And he was still alive to talk about it.

David told Levitt to select a location other than the Drake Hotel for their meeting. "Somewhere that Perilli would not feel totally comfortable, outdoors in the open." After a moment of reflection, David said, "Lincoln Park Zoo would work. I've been there with little Frankie. There's a quiet area inside the zoo grounds with picnic tables and a playground. We could sit there and discuss business. It's safe. There will be young mothers with their children playing on the park's swing sets, while we talk business. I'm certain Perilli will feel uncomfortable and that is what I want him to be - out of his element, not hidden away in the back booth of a snooty men's cocktail lounge, but out in the open for everyone to see."

Levitt responded, "That's a good idea. I'll try to set it up."

"You can also tell Jimmy that I will host him and his brother for dinner at the restaurant of their choosing, assuming we resolve all issues to my satisfaction."

"I doubt he will like the idea of meeting at the Zoo, but we'll see. I'll call Jimmy Perilli later this morning and work on getting a meeting set up," Levitt assured David.

"Set the meeting for next Wednesday at three in the afternoon," David said firmly.

"Will do, boss," Levitt replied agreeably. He was both impressed by, and worried about, David's brashness in expecting he could dictate terms to the Perillis.

"You might also suggest he dress casually rather than wearing a dark business suit, as guys like him tend to do. We won't appear too conspicuous, if we are casually dressed. Agreed?"

Levitt nodded his assent. He was surprised at the aggressiveness with which David wanted to approach hardened gangsters. *Well, I hope the kid has the moxie to pull this off,* he thought. *While it's true the Perillis need us to be able to launder their illegal profits, David seems to think they are at our mercy. That's certainly a different approach from his father's.*

"Oh, another thing," David said as they arose from the table. "Just so you understand, I don't respect the Perillis, but that doesn't mean I won't do business with them, if we can continue making lots of money dealing with them. I've reviewed this year's accounting records and things look very good. I'm willing to deal with mobsters, but on my terms, not theirs. And, I don't want to be around them or socialize with them, but I will not hesitate to take their money. Their money is just as green as the next guy's."

* * *

Levitt and Weiss arrived at the Lincoln Park Zoo at two in the afternoon on the following Wednesday. Levitt parked the car and they walked toward the playground area. It was a hot, sunny day, but there was a slight breeze off Lake Michigan that cooled the heat of the day. Weiss took a short walk around the Zoo looking at the animals in their cages. Levitt waited for Jimmy Perilli at a picnic table in the far corner of the playground. There were only a few people in the park and just one woman and two small children in the playground area. At two forty-five, Weiss returned and joined Levitt. Both men sat on one side of the picnic table. The other side they left for Jimmy Perilli and his brother.

Just before three, two large Italian men, dressed casually, appeared in the distance heading toward the playground. David looked at Levitt and asked, "Is that the Perillis?"

Levitt nodded his head and said, "The bigger one is Jimmy and the smaller one is his brother, Joe. His nickname is Little Joey. He won't say a word. Jimmy Perilli is called The Fist, because he's been known to knock out or kill men with one punch. He does all the talking for his crew."

"Interesting," Weiss said with a sarcastic smile. "I can't wait to meet them."

When the two men arrived at the picnic table, Levitt and David stood up. Levitt introduced David to them. They shook hands and sat down at the table. Jimmy and Joe Perilli immediately offered their condolences to David for the passing of his father. They inquired whether or not their large funeral spray arrived at the residence.

David assured them that it had and, thanked them for being so thoughtful.

Jimmy spread his hands and launched into a long discourse about how sorry he was about the unexpected death of his long-time friend and business associate. Jimmy related how he and Benjamin first met and he went on to describe several anecdotes about what a great guy David's father was and how the relationship between the Weiss and Perilli families had brought prosperity to both families.

David listened patiently, but as Jimmy's encomium to his father wound down, he immediately brought up the real reason for the meeting. "Mr. Perilli, ..."

"No, no, you must call me Jimmy."

"Okay, Jimmy. I understand my father was hesitant about continuing our unique business arrangements with you. I on the other hand, am not. As you say, we have all profited from doing business together. You have been a source of significant revenue for the bank, and Weiss Financial has provided a valuable service for you. It would be foolish to jeopardize such a mutually beneficial relationship."

Both Perillis were nodding and smiling with satisfaction at David's words.

He went on, "Mr. Levitt has drafted a new agreement

that I would like you to sign, which should resolve any issues that are currently problematic to us. Please look over the documents, sign them, and then we can go eat at whichever restaurant you prefer in Lincoln Park or downtown Chicago."

Jimmy Perilli looked back and forth at David and Robert Levitt in obvious surprise as Levitt passed him a multi-page document. He had anticipated having to threaten the young man, given Benjamin's stated concern about wanting to keep David in the dark about the nefarious side of the bank's business. So, Jimmy was surprised by the young man's bold approach and frankness. But he immediately liked the young man for his style and tone.

Jimmy took the document from Levitt, and huddled with Joe as they read through it. When they finished, Jimmy asked several questions, which Levitt answered. He gave David a penetrating look, and then glanced at Joe, who nodded. Jimmy signed the document and slid it across the table to Levitt. His broad face broke into a wide grin as he stretched out a hand to David. As David gripped his hand, Jimmy said, "I'm happy to put this behind us."

During the drive back to Grassville, Levitt couldn't help wondering again whether Jimmy Perilli might have played some role in Benjamin Weisses death. He was now convinced that he'd made a wise decision not to mention any such speculation to David. He was also convinced that the decision to send David Weiss to New York City to learn the business had turned out to be a brilliant move. The young man had learned even more than what his father had expected of him. Levitt always thought Benjamin was shrewd and sharp, but after seeing David's performance with the Perillis, in which he played them like a Suzuki violin, he knew David was even sharper and smarter than the elder Weiss.

Chapter 19

It was a rainy, Tuesday morning when David Weiss walked into his father's former office. Rain with thunder and lightning was predicted for the entire day. David was pleased with the progress being made in the transfer of ownership in Weiss Financial Group to him. Each day he felt more comfortable working with Robert Levitt as his advisor and the COO of Weiss Financial. They negotiated a renewal of Levitt's contract with the company, which reaffirmed the basic terms he'd worked under for many years. Angelina's pregnancy was going well and the Perilli problem seemed to be fading into the background. David's confidence in his role as the company's CEO grew daily as he got a firmer grasp on all of its operations. Miriam had come out of her funk. She told David that she was beginning to feel like her life still had purpose helping Angelina with Frankie and the pregnancy. Both Angelina and David were happy to be back in Grassville living in the mansion where David was raised from birth.

A small pile of letters and documents on the corner of his desk demanded David's attention. Yesterday was a hectic day for David; visiting several branch banks, meeting their managerial staffs, and conferring with Levitt. He could only accomplish so much in one day. As David scanned through the stack of letters, he noticed a conspicuous looking envelope. The address was composed of individual words cut out from newspapers or magazines and glued on the envelope. *Strange, why would anyone take the time and trouble to do such a thing?* David opened the envelope and to his amazement discovered a note with words cut out of newspapers and magazines glued on a white sheet of paper. The note was addressed not only to him, but to all of the members of the secret pact group.

David's hands trembled with apprehension as he read the short note. The author demanded that the recipients collectively pay one million dollars in cash by the following Monday or else information about the murder of Joel Dalton would be turned over to the police. As the letter dropped from David's shaking hand, he began to feel nauseous and weak. He weakly reached for the pitcher of water on the coffee/tea set on the credenza behind his desk. He quickly took several gulps of water, but the nausea increased. David rushed to the private bathroom inside the office and threw up his breakfast.

After he finished vomiting, David cleaned himself up and eased his body back onto the padded swivel chair behind his mahogany desk. After resting his head between his hands and carefully controlling his breathing, David began to feel better. A few minutes later, what he felt was a kindling anger. *Who in this town would dare to try to blackmail me and my friends?*

Within a few hours, David received panicked telephone

calls from all the other members of "the Pact". Each of them had received a note like his. Angelina's note was addressed to her former residence. It was the same story for the rest of the group. *So, the blackmailer must not have their current addresses,* David thought. *Here's a clue about the blackmailer. He – or, I suppose it could be a she - knew us, and where we lived, when we were in high school. The blackmailer doesn't know our current addresses; except, in my case he knew to send it to my office. Hmm.*

David called each member of the Pact back to arrange an emergency meeting at the Weiss mansion on Wednesday morning. All of them attended. After about an hour of discussion, the consensus was that David should respond to the blackmailer and negotiate his or her silence. It was agreed that the members would each contribute what he or she could afford to the final pay off. But David agreed he would bear the initial burden to pay whatever amount he worked out with the blackmailer, and then the others could reimburse him an equitable share. David was clearly better situated to handle negotiations and pay off a blackmailer than any of the others. He promised to keep them informed of his progress. He also urged all of them to continue with their lives as normal. He would not inform the authorities of the attempted blackmail and no one should contact the police about the threat. The group members left the meeting feeling relieved that David would take care of the mess.

As David thought through how to approach negotiating with a blackmailer, he had to admit to himself that covering up murder and dealing with a blackmailer was not exactly within his area of expertise. So, he turned to the person who he had come to trust as his advisor, Robert Levitt. Thus, David violated the pact made by the group of six friends and enlisted Levitt's help.

After David finished telling Levitt the story of how Joel Dalton was killed the night of the senior class prom in the parking lot, his body was dumped in the Whitcomb woods, and the group of six made a secret pact, Levitt just stared at him for a moment in startled, silent contemplation. He was amazed that the "accidental murder" had not leaked out, given that six teenagers were involved. Levitt did recall the missing-person case of the Dalton boy, but thought his father was fingered for whatever happened to the son.

Levitt cleared his throat and said, "David, I'm glad you came to me for advice rather than trying to handle this yourself. This is not the first time Weiss Financial has received a blackmail threat, and it might not be the last."

David looked sharply at Levitt, but then grunted and nodded. He recognized that the shadier side of the business might generate all sorts of threats he never imagined his father had to deal with.

Levitt continued, "The first challenge is to find out the identity of the blackmailer. The second is to eliminate the author of the notes."

David's eyes widened in surprise at the implication of Levitt's plan. *Another person has to be murdered to get us out of this mess!*

Levitt accurately read the look in David's eyes. So, he did his best to assure his young charge that this is the way these types of problems are solved in the league David now played in. "Blackmailers are seedy people and can never be trusted," Levitt said coldly. "Our friends in Chicago, the Perilli's, are much better equipped to handle the dirty work required. They are experts in making this kind of threat go away. But first, our job is to find out who the blackmailer is. Once we have a name, Jimmy Perilli will permanently solve the problem for us."

David suppressed a gasp and tried to control the tremor in his voice. "Uh, has Perilli done this kind of work for, uh, the company before?"

"Yes, he's very good at solving problems. Your father and I..." Levitt stopped mid-sentence and gave David a sympathetic look. He hated to rip the last shred off the idealized image he knew David held onto about his father.

But David looked the older man straight in the eye and then asked, "Were you about to say that my father has used Perilli to kill people in the past?"

"Well, let's just say your father was never directly involved. However, Jimmy Perilli has been a useful resource in solving some of our, shall we say, more unconventional problems over the years." Levitt gave David an assessing look trying to gauge how ready he was to learn about the most heinous activities Benjamin Weiss had involved himself in. "Since you met them, I'm sure you can't be too surprised that the Perillis have been known to eliminate people under certain circumstances."

David inhaled deeply. "Well, I guess I have to admit I'm not surprised that Jimmy and his brother, Joe, would use lethal force, if it was necessary." David shrugged and said with a slight smile, "That is what mobsters do, isn't it?"

Levitt observed the change in David's attitude and was, once again, impressed with how quickly the young man, who had the reputation of being such a straight arrow, was adapting to the ways of the "real world" Benjamin Weiss and Robert Levitt inhabited. "Yes, that is what they do, when necessary."

The seething anger David initially felt after digesting the threat the blackmailer posed had settled into a harsh, cold commitment to deal with the threat in whatever way would eliminate it forever. He told Levitt he didn't need to dance around the subject. He wholeheartedly agreed with Levitt's assessment of how the Perillis would be useful in terminating the threat.

Levitt nodded in appreciation. "So, back to our plan - I need you to compile all the information you can remember about the incident. Think carefully and try to remember every detail no matter how insignificant it might seem. Our search for the blackmailer cannot begin until we have all the facts that might serve as clues to unmask him." Levitt told David he should confer with each member of the group to find out anything they remembered or knew that he didn't.

Levitt and David agreed to meet on that same evening, following the Wednesday morning emergency gathering between David and his friends. Levitt thought about getting out of Grassville for an evening at his favorite restaurant which might help to de-stress his young boss. So, he offered to take David out to Scala Vinoteca, a popular Bedford, Indiana, Greek restaurant owned by the Lykaios family. Levitt would pick up David at seven p.m. at the mansion. Levitt said, "There is a small private dining area, near the back of the restaurant. I'll call and reserve the space for our dinner meeting."

David nodded his assent and said, "Let's get it done."

Then, their conversation turned to the more mundane and ordinary business of Weiss Financial. "It's probably time to begin implementing the plan to expand the banking operation to the southern rural Indianapolis area," Levitt suggested. "What do you think, David?"

David was happy to refocus on the sorts of issues he had prepared himself to deal with when he committed to joining the family business. "Let's visit the site first, study Indiana's developmental roadway plans, and look at the population studies surrounding the proposed branch bank in Martinsville. If everything looks good, then I think we can contact a building contractor and begin construction on our newest branch bank," David replied enthusiastically.

Chapter 20

Levitt's black Mercedes Benz pulled into the driveway of the Weiss mansion just before seven p.m. Wednesday night. David was waiting for Levitt under the portico. He opened the car door and settled into the tanned, leather passenger seat. David snapped on the seatbelt and thanked Levitt for driving.

A half hour later, Levitt pulled into the parking lot of Scala Vinoteca. "They serve wonderful five-course meals here," Levitt said. "It's my favorite place to eat."

"If it is that good, I wonder why I've never eaten here before."

"Your father preferred the Lykaios' restaurant in downtown Grassville, the Villa Capri. Your dad never liked to drive very far for dinner." Levitt chuckled. "When he was ready to eat, he wanted to eat, not drive half an hour, even if the food was better."

The men were greeted by a pretty, young hostess who led them to the private dining room reserved for their dinner meeting. After they were seated and handed menus by a server, David asked, "Are there any specialties?" He went on conversationally, "This is my first time here. I skipped breakfast and only had a chicken sandwich for lunch. So frankly, I'm starving," he said with an engaging smile to the statuesque waitress. While she listed the day's specials and made a couple recommendations, David gazed around the small private room. There were two, six-place round tables and chairs, an elegantly made mahogany serving cabinet with a glass mirror, and a glass crystal chandelier. "Private Dining Room" was embossed on a brass sign affixed to the door.

While they waited for the waitress to return with their drink orders, Levitt said, "Their fresh seafood is the best in Southern Indiana. I'd recommend it."

"It's one of my favorites," Weiss replied smiling with delight. "They serve great fresh seafood in New York City, so I've been spoiled. I doubt what I got used to in New York can be matched in southern Indiana."

"I'll let you be the judge of that," said Levitt. "Allow me to order for us, alright?"

"Sure, that's perfectly fine," David said gratefully.

When the waitress returned to take their orders, Levitt asked, "Do you still have the fresh seafood marinara on the menu?"

"Yes, we do. We just received our fresh seafood shipment today. I'd love to have our chef make the marinara for you. It's very popular with our best customers," she said with a coquettish grin.

"Well, we certainly see eye to eye on that subject," Levitt said returning her grin. "Your chef has never failed me." He nodded at David and continued, "We'd each like your Greek salad and two combination seafood marinara dinners, please."

"Excellent! Would you gentlemen like anything else?"

"No, thank you." Levitt turned and asked David if he wanted another drink.

"No, thanks. When I'm in a business meeting, I limit myself to one drink."

Levitt smiled inwardly, thinking how different the son was from the father in several respects, but just muttered, "Hmm, probably wise."

David removed two sheets of paper from a file folder and handed one to Levitt and placed the other beside his drink glass. "I think I have identified all the possible suspects. This is a list of persons that could be the blackmailer, based on the information I've gathered so far." He continued as Levitt scanned the list of names. "Of course, Angelina and I are not included on the list. But, the other four members of the 'secret pact' could have a motive. They might need cash or have something against me or one of the other members of the group. But I've known most of them since kindergarten, and all of them since middle school." David then related the history of his relationship with each of the four members of the Pact and sketched their biographies for Levitt. "I've always thought I could trust my life with each of them."

Levitt heaved a sigh, and then suggested that everyone has a price and everyone has a weakness. "Let's consider what could motivate any of your friends to betray the other members of the group." Just then, the door to the private dining room opened and a different server, a tall, slender, young man with slicked-back, black hair entered with a serving tray filled with food. The aroma caused David's empty stomach to almost leap with anticipation of the delicious-looking offerings. The waiter placed exquisite, glass-etched dinner plates in front of the two diners and laid a variety of seafood specialties on the table. "We serve this entree family style," he said. "Please let me know, if you gentlemen require anything else. Our staff will respect your privacy, while you dine. Just ring the bell I'm leaving here." He placed a small brass bell on the corner of the table by Levitt's right elbow. "And I will be at your service. If I can tempt you with dessert, tonight's special is rum cake. It looks divine. Gentlemen." The waiter executed a courtly bow, turned on his heel, and exited.

As the two men began eating their dinners, they discussed possible motives for each of the four members of the Pact. But they could not discern a likely motive for any one of the four. Howard White, Steven Mills, Staci Lykaios, and Ann Gottlieb were getting on well in life. Not one of them could be desperate for money to the extent David was aware of their financial situations. And, since each of them had at least some culpability as an accessory to a crime, why would one of them risk threatening the whole group with blackmail? That might scare a member enough to go to the authorities. No, both men agreed it would be unlikely that any member of the Pact sent the blackmail note. Nevertheless, Levitt offered to hire a private investigator to make sure that each of the four can be removed from the list of suspects.

By the time their speculation about why one of the group might break the Pact was exhausted, Weiss and Levitt had devoured the seafood marinara, finished a bottle of wine, and were ready to consider whether their engorged and satisfied stomachs could handle dessert. David patted his stomach and told Levitt he now understood why he loved this restaurant. "The food is marvelous and the staff is well trained and discrete."

Levitt smiled in appreciation and agreement, and asked, "Shall I ring the bell for dessert?"

"Why not? We might as well gorge ourselves until we burst," David said while pretending to groan with pain. Levitt tinkled the bell and the ingratiating waiter immediately appeared and took their order. Before he returned, a wisp of a young, Hispanic man with a white apron around his waist expertly cleared the dishes from the table.

After the waiter returned with a large slice of Rum Cake for each of them, David said, "There is one thing about the, uh, incident with Joel Dalton that still bothers me, and that's why his name is on the list. We checked Dalton's vitals before abandoning his body in the Whitcomb woods. Howard and I were pretty drunk, but Dalton was dead, that's for certain."

"And so?" Levitt looked at the younger man quizzically.

"What's bothering me is, why was his body never found?" David paused and gave Levitt a meaningful look. "We figured the body would eventually be discovered. It wasn't that well-hidden, and lots of hikers roam around Whitcomb Woods. We just hoped it would take long enough we'd all be off to college and there'd be no reason to suspect any of us, since no one saw us beat him up or drive away with his body."

Levitt interrupted. "Dead men don't just get up and walk away. Are you speculating that someone found the body, figured out who killed him, and is now blackmailing you?" Levitt finished in a scoffing tone, "That seems unlikely."

"I know, I know. But what we don't know is what's happened to the body. Remember, the missing person case was never solved."

"Right, the father, Lowell Dalton, was the primary suspect, but the case was closed, because Joel never turned up battered and bruised, or dead, as the police had expected."

"Yes, and now Lowell Dalton is dead too, so there would be even less reason for anyone to still be looking into that case. But what if one of the investigative officers found something that did tie us to the murder? Is it possible one of the cops did find the body, waited until I took over the company, so he'd know I could afford to pay off a blackmailer..."

"I see where you're going with this idea," Levitt cut in. "I'll also have our private investigator discretely look into the missing person case of Joel Dalton. While it's true that dead men don't get up and walk away, stranger things have happened. So, we need to find out whether Joel Dalton's body was ever discovered."

With their over-stuffed bellies, both men were ready to call it a night. Levitt asked David if he enjoyed the meal. David admitted that, "Surprisingly, this meal is as good or better than meals I've had in famous New York City restaurants." David added smiling and shaking his head, "What is this place doing in Bedford, Indiana? I can't believe it."

On the drive home, David speculated, "In my opinion, the most likely candidate as the blackmailer is someone unrelated to the Pact. The more I think about it, the more likely it seems that there was an unknown witness to Joel Dalton's beating and his accidental death. Maybe there was somebody we didn't see or notice in the parking lot. Or, maybe the blackmailer is one of my other one hundred and fifty-four classmates that attended the prom, or, maybe one of their dates." David shook his head in bewilderment.

"God, I hope you're wrong about that. With that many people to investigate, it might take weeks to find a likely suspect."

David looked anxiously over at Levitt, who had tightened his grip on the steering wheel. He replied, "I hope you don't think it could take more than a few days to end this. I'm not going to live with the threat of blackmail or jail hanging over my head!"

Levitt quickly tried to calm David and said soothingly, "No, I don't think it's going to take us that long to bring this ugly matter to a close. We'll find the identity of the would-be blackmailer, and then Jimmy Pirelli will know what to do about it." Levitt reached over the gear shift and gently patted his young boss' knee. "Don't worry, our PI is the best. And I think you now know the Pirellis well enough to be confident they will make sure you and your friends never hear from the blackmailer again." While Levitt was impressed with David's business acumen, he was worried this additional pressure on the young CEO might be too much for him to handle. He realized that he needed to tread carefully to maintain the trust and confidence David had so far placed in him.

David nodded gravely, but then became agitated again. "If we can't find out who the blackmailer is pretty soon, we'll have to wait for him to contact us. Once he does, maybe he'll screw up and make it easier for us to identify him!" His skin color had turned pale. David looked out the window of the Mercedes, and intoned in a low voice, "You know, Robert, if this doesn't end well for me, it's not going to end well for you either."

Levitt's grip on the steering wheel tightened, but his voice was mellifluous as ever as he replied, "David, there's no need for that. I said it will be taken care of and it will be."

Instead of being placated, David's impatience and agitation increased as the Mercedes neared his home. "Maybe Howard and I should go back out to the Whitcomb Woods and check out the site, where we left the body, see if it's still there or been disturbed. That might tell us whether somebody has found it. I don't want to just sit around waiting!"

Levitt shot a nervous glance in David's direction, but

decide it was best not to interrupt David's rant. He obviously needed to let off the nervous tension that had been building inside him. Levitt had hoped that fine dining with wine would help to ease the mental strain on his young boss, but it seemed to be having the opposite effect on the drive back to the Weiss mansion.

"Howard White and I were the only ones that were in the woods that night, as far as we knew. When we, uh, you know, left Dalton's corpse there." David shot a glance at Levitt to judge his reaction, but saw his advisor's face remained impassive. "I'm not even sure I can remember the exact spot, but Howard knows the woods pretty well. He used to trail run in the woods training for track and cross-country. I'm sure he can find the place where we covered the body."

Levitt calmly said, "You know, by now the remains will likely be no more than bones. There must be animals and insects that would have consumed most, if not all of the body. There might be some bits of clothing left."

"True enough," David acknowledged.

To try to divert David from what Levitt thought was a bad idea – his young boss tromping around in Whitcomb Woods looking for the body of the boy he murdered – Levitt took the conversation in a different direction. "Too bad the father is not still alive, isn't it?" David just grunted in response. But Levitt persisted. "You said his father was an ex-con, bully, career criminal, who supposedly beat him on a regular basis, right?"

"Yes, that's correct, David acknowledged.

"Maybe someone knew about how badly the boy was being abused by his father, who was a known criminal."

"So?" David evinced little interest in pursuing this line of inquiry, as it seemed literally and figuratively a dead end.

"What if he had a guardian angel, so to speak, that was trying to watch over him?" Levitt began to warm to his own idea. *Hmm*, he thought, *this actually might be worth pursuing.*

David nearly barked his response, "So what if he did! If somebody wanted to protect Joel from his father, they did a piss poor job of it, from what I know. But the old man got what he deserved anyway. He was assassinated by another inmate at the Indiana State Prison in Michigan City, Indiana, five or six years ago. So why would any so-called guardian angel want to come after us, if they thought the old man was the perpetrator?" David asked disgustedly.

Continuing in a calm tone, Levitt said, "But what if someone watching out for Joel was there at the Prom waiting to pick him up? It didn't have to be a social worker or a cop." Levitt paused thoughtfully, "Did Joel have any friends, maybe someone older, like a big brother or big sister type?"

"Nobody liked Joel Dalton!" David nearly spat it out.

"Okay, so he didn't have any friends to speak of at school, but were there any older figures in his life that might have felt sorry for him and might have wanted to try to protect him from his father?"

David took a deep breath. He realized he was losing

control. And that was something he never wanted to do. His years of athletic training and the rigid expectations of his father had created a steely self-discipline. He knew how to maintain a firm grip on his emotions now, just like when it was fourth and long in a close football game. He concentrated for a moment, and then said in an even, almost submissive tone, "Well, Lowell Dalton was known to have a girlfriend. I don't recall her first name, but I think her last name was Morgan." David turned and looked hopefully at Levitt, "Maybe she took an interest in Joel, like you're suggesting."

"What do we know about her?" Levitt asked curiously.

"Not very much, I'm afraid. The rumor was she's a former stripper, prostitute, drug addict, and alcoholic. Not exactly the perfect resume for a guardian angel," David said with a sarcastic laugh. "Apparently, for some reason she loved Lowell Dalton. They say at one time she was quite a looker. The locals were surprised she'd hooked up with Dalton, a dangerous thug, drug dealer, and ex-con. But she was from out of town, so she might not have known about his past."

"Let's put her name on our list of people to talk to. Even though she doesn't sound like the Mother Teresa type, who knows, she might know something worth finding out." Levitt nodded with satisfaction. "Our PI will be able to locate her, and find out what she thought of Joel Dalton and what she was doing the night he, uh, became a missing person case," Levitt said delicately.

It was ten thirty when David finally opened the door of the Mercedes to step out in front of the portico at the Weiss mansion. He was tired and told Levitt they could resume their discussion the following day. Levitt nodded his assent, put the car in gear, and slowly drove away.

Chapter 21

On Thursday morning at six a.m., Levitt left a message on Edwin Cranston's answering machine in Chicago, Illinois. The message was simple, "This is Robert Levitt in Grassville, Indiana, calling. I have an emergency job for you. Please call me at your earliest convenience." Levitt had retained Cranston for Weiss Financial several times in the last five years.

In the course of Edwin Cranston's career, he had been a U.S. Foreign Service officer, FBI agent, and, was now a well-known Las Vegas private investigator. Cranston left the FBI as a highly decorated and renowned agent, when his wife became sick with terminal breast cancer. When Liz Cranston died, Cranston used alcohol therapy to ease the pain. He began drinking during Liz's slow and agonizing fight with cancer. After she passed, he totally succumbed to the bottle. His drink of choice was a shot of whiskey, followed by a glass of beer. After hiding his alcoholism from the Bureau for six months, it became too obvious and he was forced to resign as an agent. When his FBI career was over, he began to have suicidal thoughts. A former FBI agent and friend helped to sober Cranston up three years after his resignation. Cranston began attending AA meetings, recognized and admitted his problem, and gave up drinking. He was sober for the past seven years.

Once he was sober and could work again, Cranston quickly developed a highly lucrative specialty as a private investigator working exclusively for casino operations in Las Vegas, Nevada. His job was to find gamblers, who ran off and tried to get away with not paying their gambling debts. Some gambling high-rollers, and some smaller fish gambling-addicts, thought they could get away with not paying off their debts by hiding out for a while. But the casino bosses didn't forget or forgive gambling debts so easily. So, they turned to Cranston to locate the welchers. When he found them, Cranston informed the corporate financial departments of the casinos. The casinos would then, if necessary, employ men like the Perillis, who were skilled in the art of persuasion, to handle the collection process of the unpaid debt.

Cranston also offered his services to private clients, upon request. Clients like Levitt, who dealt with sensitive matters for their bosses. Cranston was well paid for his services in Las Vegas, but investigations for clients outside of Las Vegas paid even better. Edwin Cranston, lived most of his adult life in Alexandra, Virginia. But he moved to Chicago, where he rented a lake-side luxury apartment on the Outer Drive, overlooking the skyline of downtown Chicago, after his PI business really took off.

Three hours after Levitt left the message on Cranston's answering machine in his Chicago apartment, Cranston returned the call. "Good morning, Mr. Levitt, this is Edwin

Cranston returning your call," Cranston politely said. "What kind of job do you have for me this time?"

Levitt immediately replied, "Good morning, Mr. Cranston. I have a job that demands your complete discretion and an immediate response. I'm going to give you some names of people I want you to investigate. However, you must not tip off any of these people that they're being investigated. These individuals are close friends of my boss. They are all originally from Grassville, Indiana. Their names are Howard White, Staci Lykaios, Steven Mills, and Ann Gottlieb."

"Okay," Cranston said as he wrote the four names on a yellow-lined note pad. "Where are they now?"

"Howard White is attending Law School at Harvard in Cambridge, Massachusetts. Staci Lykaios is Howard's girlfriend and lives with him in Cambridge. Steven Mills went to school in Muncie, Indiana at Ball State University, but is now running a large hardware store in Vincennes, Indiana with his father. Ann Gottlieb went to college at the University of Notre Dame and now works as an elementary school teacher for at-risk children, in a public school in South Bend, Indiana," Levitt said carefully articulating the information to Cranston.

"Okay, I've jotted down that information. But what do you want to know about those people?"

"My boss wants to know about their financial backgrounds and if you can find any dirt on any of them. The reason behind these inquiries is confidential. Be extra thorough on these folks, because it involves trust issues.

Understand?" Levitt ended emphatically.

"Yes, sir," Cranston replied crisply. "I assume you want me to get started immediately."

"That is correct, but I've got two other names of people I want you to investigate." Levitt continued, "The first one will be difficult and confusing, but I want you to see what you can find out about Joel Dalton, also of Grassville, Indiana. Once you get into his investigation you will discover why I am describing this search as difficult and confusing. Regardless, pursue this investigation to the very end. Joel Dalton has been missing since June 4, 1988. He was last seen in Grassville, Indiana. His whereabouts is currently unknown. His deceased father was accused of killing him, but a body was never found. Lowell Dalton died in prison. He was convicted of unrelated charges, but after his death the police dropped the investigation and the case remains unsolved.

There is also a woman we'd like you to find. Her last name is Morgan. She was Lowell Dalton's girlfriend. Lowell was the father to Joel, but he is dead, as I've previously stated. Lowell was killed at the Indiana State Penitentiary in Michigan City, Indiana, by an assassin settling a dispute between a Hispanic gang and the deceased. I'll be sending you via facsimile all of the subjects' biographical information that we have, within the hour. This is very important to my boss and I want your assurance that these investigations will begin today."

"I'll start on them as soon as I wrap up my current job, which should only take me a few more hours." Cranston paused to do a quick calculation in his head, then grunted softly, "Uh huh. I'll expect my usual advance fee of $10,000 plus an additional bonus of $5,000. I'll credit the advance at the rate of $1,000 per day, and I'll bill you for my expenses and any overage beyond the advance. Is that agreeable?"

"That sounds fine to me. We appreciate your help once again," Levitt replied gravely. "Once you've started the investigation, call me anytime, if you need more information from us."

Following the conversation with Cranston, Levitt called Weiss to report that the investigations into the people on the list would commence within a few hours. Levitt was pleased to note the sound of relief in Weiss' voice. He was even more pleased when Weiss apologized for getting over-excited on the drive home from Scala Vinoteca. Levitt assured his young boss he'd taken no offense. What had made a deeper impression on the older man was David Weiss' willingness to expose his darker side. A side which Levitt did not know even existed, until the meeting in Chicago with the Perilli brothers. But it was now clear that the young CEO's exposure to Cousin Walter Kohen had changed him indelibly from the all-American sports star and scholar that Levitt had known as the adolescent David Weiss.

Levitt was beginning to believe the similarities between David Weiss and Benjamin Weiss were much greater than what he'd originally thought. The son appeared to be much tougher, but less flexible and less reasonable, than his father had been. Levitt still felt secure in his position with Weiss Financial, but he realized he'd have to watch his every move. David Weiss reminded him of the type of person, who would do anything to survive, including firing his most trusted advisor, if trust in that advisor was lost. *Perhaps that's why David was such a good quarterback,* Levitt mused. *His defensive mechanisms and maneuvers probably came natural to him.*

Levitt asked Weiss if he wanted to further discuss the subject of last night's meeting. Weiss said that he did, and they should meet at two p.m. at the mansion. When Levitt arrived, Weiss announced his plan to go back to Whitcomb woods with Howard White in tow. He said he'd already discussed his plan with White and White agreed to catch the next flight to Indianapolis early Friday morning. Weiss would arrange for a driver to meet White at the airport and drive him to the mansion. He and White would drive to the woods later in the afternoon. They would make it look like they were just out for a challenging hike on the trails through Whitcomb Woods, while they searched for Dalton's corpse.

Levitt was shocked but not surprised. He urged David to reconsider. "Visiting the woods could be a dangerous and unnecessary step. What if, God forbid, someone sees you in the woods digging around in the dirt early in the afternoon? Have you really thought this through?"

"I don't see the danger for us walking in the woods," David replied haughtily. "Besides, if we find something like a skull or frayed clothing, we'll have our answer as to the whereabouts of Joel Dalton. And, it will be very unlikely that we'll encounter anyone in the woods on a Friday afternoon."

"David, I thought that was the reason for hiring the PI. I am trying to shield you from any potential risk. My job is to protect you and to steer you away from making a bad decision. In my view, going to the woods would not be in your best interests," Levitt replied insistently.

"Robert, I appreciate your concern. I know you are genuinely concerned about my welfare, and I think you're doing an excellent job. However, I am willing to take a calculated risk, if I think it will be helpful. If Howard and I can spend a minimal amount of time in the woods early tomorrow afternoon and put the Joel Dalton mystery to rest, I think the risk is worth it," Weiss said flatly.

Levitt realized it was useless to further debate the issue, so he backed down, just shaking his head, and said, "Okay David, I hope it works out for the best." But he still believed it was not a smart move.

* * *

Howard White drove to the woods the following afternoon, with David in the passenger seat beside him. David couldn't help wondering whether his decision was the correct one. Levitt had cautioned him to try not to look suspicious while digging around for any signs of Dalton's body. If someone saw the two men and asked what they were looking for buried deep within the woods, how should he answer? The cover story he told Howard he thought they should employ was to say they were burying a dead pet. David had doubts that would be very convincing to a suspicious mind, but it was the best answer he'd thought of, and Howard hadn't come up with a better one.

It was a muggy day. The sunlight was bright and the temperatures were in the mid-eighties. White turned the corner a mile from the woods and in the distance saw something he didn't expect to see. He stopped at the corner and checked the road signs. White verified he was on the correct road heading toward the woods. Startled, he punched David, who was slumped to the right side of the passenger seat, trying to get some much-needed rest. The blackmail notes and his worrying about who was responsible had disrupted his normal sleeping pattern. White yelled, "What the hell!" David stirred and looked in the direction Howard was pointing. A housing development under construction sprawled out and into what had been the Whitcomb Woods. A few islands of undisturbed woodland remained within the gigantic new subdivision. Howard drove slowly by the gated entrance as the two friends gaped at the scene of deforestation and new construction.

On the drive back to the mansion, David apologized to his old friend for having him return to Grassville on a wild goose chase. White was unaware of the development, because he paid little attention to events in Grassville since moving to Cambridge. But David admitted he should have remembered this was the location of a major new development project by an Indianapolis real estate development firm. He shook his head wearily, and blamed his inattention on focusing on getting control of the family business, since moving back from New York City. "Sorry

Howard, I should have realized the new subdivision was going in at Whitcomb Woods. It's not financed by Weiss Financial. The developer, Johnson Bros., is a large Indianapolis firm who's financed through Chase Manhattan Bank." David's irritation that his COO, Robert Levitt, was either unaware of the development or had decided to teach David some kind of perverted lesson by not telling him that Whitcomb Woods no longer existed. *Surely Levitt, who has his pulse on everything around town, knew about this, so did he forget, or is he playing some kind of game with me?* David's father's advice to trust no one hummed in his brain.

If a body had been discovered during the grading, utility installations, and the paving portion of the development, it would have been in the news. Likewise, if a body was found during the housing construction phase of the project, it would have made the local headlines. David was sure he would have been alerted to any news of Dalton's remains being discovered, so he had to conclude no evidence of a corpse was found in the woods. He wasn't sure what to make of this, but one thing he intended to get straight was why Levitt hadn't informed him that the woods had been cleared.

When Howard dropped David off back at the mansion, he made a bee-line for the phone and called Robert Levitt to demand to know why Levitt hadn't warned him that the woods had been cleared. Levitt's initial reaction to David's angry tone was honest astonishment. He admitted he was aware of the development on that side of town, but didn't realize it was happening in the Whitcomb Woods. He reminded David that he was not originally from Grassville, and paid little attention to matters of purely local interest when Weiss Financial was not involved. "David, until you told me about the Joel Dalton matter, I had never even heard of Whitcomb Woods."

David seemed mollified by the end of their conversation. Levitt was actually relieved by David's report about the Whitcomb Woods Development Project and the failed adventure in the woods. *David got lucky this time,* he thought. Levitt was still annoyed that David had refused to heed his advice and had gone off half-cocked to hunt for Dalton's body, or what would be left of it. *Maybe this will be a lesson and the young buck will be more cautious in the future. I need to work on getting him to accept my suggestions, instead of rashly charging ahead without proper intelligence and planning. Still, I do admire the young CEO's guts, persistence, and drive.*

Levitt considered calling Edwin Cranston to share the news about the Whitcomb Woods, and then to explain that's where the body of Joel Dalton, one of the names on the list, had supposedly been dumped. But he decided against sharing that information with the PI. That Joel Dalton was killed by Levitt's boss and his friends was not information he needed to share, at least not yet. The lack of a body was not in itself evidence of anything other than Joel Dalton was still missing. *Let's see what Cranston discovers about him.*

Chapter 22

Levitt called Weiss at eight a.m. on Saturday morning. The topic of conversation was, again, about the details of what happened the night of the incident. Levitt was sure there must be a significant piece of information they'd missed. He was convinced someone watched as the three boys man-handled Joel Dalton in the gymnasium parking lot. But David had gone over and over that possibility with the members of the Pact. Neither he nor any of his friends could remember seeing anyone anywhere close enough to see what happened in the parking lot that night.

Still, Levitt was sure David and his friends had missed something and said so. "I've got a feeling there's more to this than what we already know."

Weiss was not convinced. He believed, if there was some piece of information they'd missed, they would have already thought of it. However, he decided, it would be wise to listen to Levitt and not disregard the older, more experienced man's views. David knew Levitt was very smart and an intuitive thinker. He had served his father well as a problem solver. Besides, it was always better to have two people thinking about solving the mystery of Joel

Dalton, rather than just one. Weiss remembered his father telling him that Levitt was a bright, ingenious man and well worth what he paid for his advice and counsel.

After reviewing once more every detail of the incident David could remember and his friends had related, Levitt tactfully encouraged his young boss to contact his friends one more time and to urge them to think about the night of the prom and the beating the boys had given Dalton. "What do we have to lose?" Levitt asked in a sincere tone. "Maybe we'll get lucky and someone will remember something important that they forgot to bring up."

Later that morning, David called all his friends one by one and drilled each of them once again on their recollections of prom night. He also asked Angelina the same set of questions. Not a single member of the "secret pact" could remember anything beyond what they already related about the incident. Weiss was disappointed, but understood that the incident happened in 1988 and they were trying to remember every detail in 1994. Six years was a long time to remember every moment about an event, especially when you and your friends were intoxicated to varying degrees at the time.

Weiss updated his friends on the progress made thus far on the ongoing investigation. He indicated a well-known and respected private investigator was working on the case. The PI's charge was to study the blackmail note and to determine who sent it. Weiss also mentioned that he and White ventured back to the Whitcomb Woods and discovered the site was now an expensive housing development under construction. He told them, "To date, there are no reports about finding the remnants of human bones or clothing by construction workers at the development." So, Joel Dalton was still considered missing. Weiss also revealed a second firm was working on finding a possible trail left by Joel Dalton. He purposely failed to mention the other firm was the Perilli Brothers.

During their afternoon meeting, Levitt shared a theory with Weiss about Joel Dalton that he'd developed. He told Weiss, "If we assume Joel's father did not kill him and that Joel was still alive, then, what happened to him?" Levitt reasoned that, if he fled Grassville to get away from his father, he probably needed to hide. But how would he hide unless he changed his identification papers? To do that would require the assistance of a professional forger to provide him with new papers, a new name, and a new past. Weiss' advisor also reasoned, at the time of his departure from Grassville, Dalton would not have had enough money to go too far. So, where would he go? The logical conclusion would be he'd go to a larger city that had more job opportunities. And, he'd probably try to distance himself from Grassville by at least a hundred miles. "If my reasoning is spot on or close," he told Weiss, "It would mean he'd go either to Indianapolis, Louisville, or St. Louis." Those were the three closest major metropolitan areas.

Weiss replied, "Dalton was undoubtedly an IU Hoosier fan, like everybody else in Grassville. So, wouldn't he most likely have made Indianapolis his first choice?"

Levitt agreed that made sense and that Indianapolis would be a good starting place to look for Joel Dalton.

Weiss instructed Levitt to contact Jimmy Perilli and ask him to start communicating with some of his underworld contacts in the Indianapolis area about the whereabouts of Joel Dalton.

Levitt immediately called Jimmy Perilli and Edwin Cranston. He explained his theory that Joel Dalton might be somewhere in the Indianapolis area. Perilli said he had some contacts in Indy and that he'd find out the names of all the forgers. "Once I've run them down," Perilli said, "I'll pay them a personal visit to see if they ever worked in 1988 for a scrawny kid by the name of Joel Dalton."

Cranston commented to Levitt that his theory seemed very believable and indicated that Indianapolis would be a good starting point to begin his search for Joel Dalton. Cranston assumed Levitt was using others in the desperate search for the Dalton kid. Levitt also reasoned that it wouldn't take much money to travel to Indianapolis, get a low-level job, rent a rundown apartment, and eke out a living. But, after six years, if Dalton was still in the same area, he'd probably have a better job and a more stable life by now.

Perilli's associate in Indianapolis, Fred Roselli, called to tell him there were two active forgers working in the Indianapolis area. The first guy Roselli contacted, Barry Simmons, claimed he'd been sick and in and out of business for the past seven years. But he recommended Roselli talk to Jason Peoples, who was a full-time forger on the northeastern side of town. Peoples was referred to by the locals as "Slim". He did his work in the basement of a rundown, old house just east of Keystone Avenue. Slim was well-known within the Indianapolis underworld. After getting off the phone with Roselli about Jason Peoples, Jimmy and Joe Perilli were soon in their car and on the way to Indianapolis."

When they arrived at People's house late Saturday afternoon, Joe Perilli climbed out of his Cadillac, approached the house, and knocked on People's front door. Peoples looked through the window shade and determined his visitor on the front porch was not a cop. He quickly answered the door and invited the two gangsters inside. The Perillis began to question Slim. At first, Peoples was quiet and decided to feel the two men out. But since they knew his nickname and what he did for a living, he decided it would be worthwhile to listen to their story.

Peoples claimed to remember a scrawny kid about five or six years earlier that he'd done work for. Slim said, "I believe, I made him an Indiana Driver's License and a local birth certificate." Perilli asked him if he remembered the kid's name. Peoples said he couldn't recall it. But after another minute of reflection, Slim remembered he'd made two birth certificates because he inscribed the wrong birth date on the first birth certificate he made. He thought he remembered saving the screwed-up one in his file folder. Slim excused himself and went to the basement to see if he'd saved the document. A few minutes later, Peoples returned with a birth certificate from Community Hospital East of Indianapolis. The name on the document was George Nelson.

Perilli called Levitt to report the information received from Peoples. Levitt was delighted to learn that Joel

Dalton had somehow survived the brutal beating inflicted on him by young Weiss and his cohorts. Whether Dalton was still alive was not yet known, but it was likely that he was and living in the Indianapolis area. The major significance of the intelligence from Slim was that David Weiss and his friends could never be charged with murder, since the Dalton boy was alive and well and obtaining forged ID papers after he'd been left for dead in the woods. This now made Joel Dalton a prime suspect as the blackmailer.

After Levitt informed Cranston of the information about Joel Dalton's existence and change of identity, the PI quickly located Dalton's current address. Cranston also discovered that Dalton was a truck driver and a rental-housing property owner. Apparently, Joel Dalton had saved and invested money wisely, because the Marion County Recorder's records showed that George Nelson owned six rental properties in Marion County. Cranston also determined that Joel Dalton, aka George Nelson, was living with a younger woman.

When Levitt advised David Weiss of the information developed by Cranston, Weiss immediately assumed that "George Nelson" must be the blackmailer and was all fired up to pay him a personal visit. Levitt cautioned his young, and once again, hot-headed boss against doing that. He argued that Perilli should handle it. "David, let the professionals do their jobs, and that way you keep your hands clean."

But David insisted that he wanted to see Nelson himself, question him, and determine if he needed to be dealt with or not. He was concerned the Perillis' might get carried away and kill him without finding out whether Nelson was, in fact, the blackmailer. David was also curious to learn how George Nelson survived the beating inflicted on Joel Dalton.

On Sunday morning, David drove to Indianapolis to pay George Nelson a visit. Robert Levitt insisted that he accompany his young charge to make sure things did not get out of hand.

When Weiss pulled up to George Nelson's modest ranch home, located in a middle-class neighborhood on Indianapolis' eastside, he wondered what Nelson would be like after six years living as a runaway with an assumed identity. Weiss and Levitt got out of their vehicle and walked up to Nelson's front door. They knocked on the door and waited for Nelson to answer.

When Joel Dalton, aka George Nelson, opened his front door, he was shocked and concerned to see David Weiss standing on his front porch. He nervously invited the two men inside his home. After a brief introduction by Weiss of Robert Levitt as his corporate attorney, Nelson pointed to the living room couch and the two men took a seat. Weiss was amazed by the changes he saw in Dalton. He remembered him as a scrawny, ill-bred hillbilly, the most unpopular kid in Grassville High. Dalton was, of course, a grown man. He was still slight of build, but was dressed in pressed blue jeans with a clean, light blue work shirt neatly tucked into his pants. The house looked a little weathered, but the lawn was mowed, and the interior quite presentable.

With a puzzled look on his face, Nelson asked Weiss apprehensively, "Mr. Weiss, why are you here and what can I do for you?"

"Well, I heard you lived in Indianapolis and I wanted to see how you are doing. It's been a long time since high school. Six years, in fact."

Both Weiss and Levitt noted that, after his initial look of shock at their appearance at his front door, Dalton was acting like a cordial host, although still perhaps a bit confused about the purpose of their visit. Weiss gave Dalton an engagingly friendly smile and asked, "Why and when did you move to Indianapolis?"

"I moved here in 1988 the day after you and your friends beat me up and left me in the woods. But I want you to know I've never held a grudge. I deserved the beating you gave me, Mr. Weiss."

"Well, you may have deserved a beating Joel, or should I call you George?" Weiss asked with a smirk, but didn't wait for a reply. "My friends and I admittedly went too far, but that is all history now." Weiss' mouth tightened, but then he relaxed again, and said in a conversational tone, "I understand you drive truck and have a handful of residential properties you rent."

A flash of fear crossed Joel's face, but then he replied in an obsequious tone of voice, "Yes, sir, I do. When I first arrived in Indianapolis it was tough to make a living, but after I earned by GED and got my CDL license my life changed for the better. I'm not the same person that you knew in high school."

"So why did you leave Grassville, George?"

"I was tired of being beaten up by my dad and having to support all his bad habits," Nelson said frankly.

"Did you have much money saved in order to make the move?" Levitt asked.

"Well, when I got home from the woods the following morning, there was an envelope full of cash waiting for me at the front door along with a short note. The note requested I leave Grassville immediately. I assumed your boss provided the cash and wrote the note." Nelson replied to Levitt, but then looked over nervously at Weiss.

Weiss immediately chimed in and said, "Sorry George, but you are mistaken. I wouldn't have left you anything at the time. Why did you find it necessary to change your name?"

"I didn't want my father to find me, beat me up, and take me back to Grassville," Nelson said with a shrug.

"I suppose you've heard that my father passed away and I am now in charge of the company."

"Yes, I read about your father's passing in the newspaper," Nelson replied with a slight touch of anxiety in his voice.

"George," Weiss said as he stared into the young man's eyes, "Did you send me and my friends a blackmail note demanding a million dollars?" Weiss and Levitt both stared at George Nelson to gauge the honesty of his response. They were disappointed to observe that Nelson appeared utterly astonished by the question. Weiss immediately concluded that George Nelson knew nothing about the attempted blackmail. Levitt, on the other hand, was not so easily convinced.

Nelson's response to the question was, "I'm not crazy! I would be too scared to ever do such a thing, particularly to you, Mr. Weiss. I've uh, heard stories about your family connections, you know. Besides, I'm not smart enough to pull something like that off. I drive a truck for a living and rent apartments to poor people. I'm no longer a thief, I've really turned my life around, and don't have anything to do with any illegal activities," Nelson asserted emphatically.

Weiss nodded his head and said, "That's a good thing, George." Then, he resumed his questioning. "What can you tell me about your father's girlfriend? I believe her last name is Morgan, but I don't know her first name."

"Uh, yeah, her name is Sally Morgan. I can't tell you very much about her, I'm afraid. She was originally from West Virginia. I haven't seen or talked to her in years," Nelson stated plainly.

"When we caught you stealing from our cars the night of the prom, did you have an accomplice?" David asked directly.

"No, not really. But Sally Morgan was waiting in the parking lot to take me home. However, the way things turned out, as you know, I didn't need a ride home," George replied with a note of resentment in his voice.

"Hmm," Weiss mused thoughtfully, then turned his head toward Levitt, who was nodding at him encouragingly. "What else can you tell us about Sally

Morgan?"

"Well, I heard that, after my father was killed in prison Sally went to his funeral service and then, a few days later, she freaked out. She was doing drugs, alcohol, and everything else you can imagine. Anyway, my source told me she tried to kill herself. The last information I got about Sally Morgan was that she was taken to Logansport, Indiana and placed in a psychiatric hospital for the criminally insane. As far as I know, she might still be there." George looked at each of the men with a wide-eyed honest expression on his face.

Hearing that, Weiss and Levitt arose from the couch. Weiss extended his hand to Nelson and said, "It was good to see you again George, and to know you are doing well. Sorry to have troubled you at home. Good luck with your rentals. And, if you ever need a loan, give us a call." The two men shook hands cordially.

George Nelson was surprised by the visit. He had hoped never to see David Weiss up close and personal again. He watched with dismay as the two men pulled away from the curb in a luxurious-looking, black Mercedes Benz. Nelson stood on his porch thoughtfully watching the Mercedes head down the street and then turn a corner to vanish from his sight.

On the ride back to Grassville, Levitt questioned Weiss as to why he was certain George Nelson wasn't the blackmailer. Weiss said that he found Nelson convincing, and that George Nelson, unlike Joel Dalton, just didn't seem like the kind of person who would come up with a blackmail scheme. Levitt said that he wanted to have

Cranston dig further into George Nelson's life before they eliminated him as a suspect. "You know, David, the apple doesn't fall far from the tree."

Weiss shrugged. Just because Dalton's father was a crook didn't mean the son had to follow in his father's footsteps. Weiss was convinced that Joel Dalton was a changed man. Sure, he understood that in Dalton's previous life he was a thief, but blackmailing a powerful executive, like himself, seemed to be too much of a stretch. Obviously, Dalton was smart enough to drive a truck and have a few rental properties, but so what. He told Levitt, "It takes a certain degree of intelligence to plan this kind of thing out and Joel Dalton was not blessed with much intelligence."

Levitt listened and nodded in agreement when Weiss mentioned Dalton's lack of intelligence. When Dalton told them proudly that he'd earned his GED and CDL license, neither of them were impressed. But Levitt wouldn't be satisfied until Cranston dug more deeply into Dalton's life. But their next move was to put Cranston to work locating Sally Morgan. He could look further into Dalton's new life as George Nelson as soon as he found Sally Morgan.

Chapter 23

Levitt didn't know who to suspect as the blackmailer. The culprit could be Joel Dalton aka George Nelson, Sally Morgan, or somebody else. Dalton placed Morgan in the parking lot the night of the prom. Levitt thought, therefore, she may very well have witnessed the incident in the parking lot. She might have seen them hauling away Joel's body in the trunk of Weiss' car and got scared, so she just took off. Or, maybe she followed the boys to the woods. David discounted that theory, when Levitt proposed it, because he was sure they were alone in the woods. On the other hand, he had to concede that it was possible neither Howard nor he noticed her, because she was careful to keep her distance. If Dalton was not at the top of the list of suspects, and none of the Pact members had risen to the top, then, they both concluded that Sally Morgan was probably their best lead.

Levitt called Cranston and asked him to switch mid-stream and concentrate his efforts on finding Sally Morgan and looking into her past, instead of looking further into Joel Dalton's elusive life. Levitt updated Cranston on Sally Morgan's location, as a patient, at the Indiana State Mental

Hospital in Logansport, Indiana.

Several hours later, Levitt received a call from Edwin Cranston. He discovered that Sally Morgan was discharged from the Indiana State Mental Hospital several months before Weiss received the blackmail note. Cranston bribed an orderly from the hospital staff, for information about her. The orderly claimed that after discharge she would have been referred to a community mental health center in the locale where she chose to live. The orderly couldn't help as to Morgan's current residence, because that information would be highly confidential and above his pay grade. So, Cranston was unable to determine where she'd gone after discharge. But the helpful orderly did say Sally Morgan's initial admission was caused by a major depression. But she must have improved enough to warrant her discharge. Although, the orderly stated, "She would be medicated, receive out-patient care, undergo group therapy, and would be under the care and supervision of a psychiatrist. He also explained that many depressed patients have cognitive functioning issues following a regimen of heavy medication during an involuntary admission, like Morgan's. But the orderly didn't think her cognitive functioning was that bad by the time of her discharge, because, as he recalled, "Sally was able to navigate the world around her pretty well."

Of course, Levitt understood that the orderly's perceptions of her mental faculties were not based on clinical information about Sally Morgan's case. He was not in her residential wing at the hospital, but he knew another orderly who took care of her. That orderly claimed she seemed to be alright. But, her considerable prior illegal drug use, the orderly admitted, could have induced some degree of psychosis. Cranston told Levitt he would continue looking for Morgan, but the prospects of finding her were currently not that good. Personal patient records were hard to get. So, Cranston did not know where to look for Sally Morgan after her discharge. The PI said he would keep trying and see what he could come up with.

Cranston was able to discover that Sally Morgan had held an Indiana driver's license, but it was expired. He also found out she previously owned a white, 1981 Pontiac sedan. Apparently, the circuit court judge who ordered her admission into the State Hospital also ordered her vehicle to be sold. Those funds were being held by her court appointed guardian, a Ms. Vivian Lantz, from Grassville, who was her former neighbor in the trailer park where she lived.

On Monday morning, Cranston approached Ms. Lantz saying that he represented the Indiana State Mental Health Commission and wanted to follow up on her care and treatment since she left the State facility. Ms. Lantz cooperated and told Cranston that Sally Morgan was living in a group home in Michigan City, Indiana. Ms. Lantz arranged a meeting with Sally for Cranston, so he could interview her the following morning.

Several hours later, David Weiss received a call from Howard White. He claimed Staci remembered what seemed like an insignificant event that occurred the night of the Prom that she had not mentioned before. According to Staci, she saw an older white, beat-up Pontiac sedan leaving the parking lot after they placed Joel's body into the trunk of David's car. At the time, she didn't think much of it, because she assumed it was one of their classmates leaving the Prom. "Since the car was at the far end of the parking lot, whoever was in it wouldn't have walked near our group during the incident," White told Weiss, "But still, it might be worth looking into. Staci feels really bad that she didn't think of this before. And, she was sorry and embarrassed to tell you herself."

Weiss thanked Howard for the information and told him to tell Staci not to worry about it. "I'm sure she tried to do her level best to remember every minute detail and I understand how difficult that can be all these years later." David said he'd check back in with Howard in a couple of days, if he thought of anything else he wanted to question Staci about.

Weiss called Levitt and informed him of the information he just received from White concerning an older, white sedan leaving the parking lot at the time of the incident. Levitt's interest in Sally Morgan as a suspect was even more piqued. And Weiss was now convinced that the blackmailer was Sally Morgan. "Remember Dalton's statement about expecting Morgan to pick him up in the parking lot, after finishing the job! Staci's recollection that an older, white sedan pulled out of the parking lot, following the beating, tracks perfectly with Dalton's statement," David concluded with satisfaction.

With the verification that Joel Dalton was alive; Weiss happily realized that the blackmailer no longer had any leverage to use against him and his friends. So that problem was resolved. But, as he mused in conversation with Levitt, the remaining questions were: Who was the blackmailer? Would the author of the note ever be found? And, what would they do to the blackmailer, if anything, once the blackmailer's identity was revealed?

Levitt knew David Weiss was cunning, vindictive, and not very predictable. He had no idea what Weiss might do to the blackmailer, if his worst instincts weren't checked. So, Levitt advised Weiss to do nothing and try to forget the anxiety the whole issue created, once the problem was resolved.

The Secret Pact

Chapter 24

On Tuesday morning, Cranston traveled to Michigan City, Indiana to conduct an interview with Sally Morgan. He told Vivian Lantz to inform Ms. Morgan that he would arrive around ten a.m. at the group home where Sally lived. The shingled two-story group home was located in the 300 block of E. 11th St. in a racially and ethnically diverse neighborhood, which had a high crime rate. Cranston drove past Michigan City on various occasions, but he had never actually been in the city. Michigan City was a working-class town, adjacent to Lake Michigan. The Indiana State Prison was a major employer. Cranston wondered whether the reason Sally Morgan wanted to live in Michigan City was because her lover and friend, Lowell Dalton, was buried there.

When Cranston arrived at the group home, several older ladies greeted him at the front door. They were frail and appeared to be somewhat mentally challenged. He asked for Sally Morgan and, without any questions or objections, but muttering to each other about Sally having a gentleman caller, they escorted him to her room and announced his presence. The women were obviously excited to have an attractive, male visitor in the home. Morgan was in a rocking chair rocking slowly back and forth. She seemed only vaguely aware of Mr. Cranston's presence, when he introduced himself to her. But when she finally looked up and saw a handsome man standing in front of her, a wide smile appeared on her face and she said, "Hello," in a raspy voice. Cranston thought this was not going to be an easy interview as this creature appeared to be in a very befuddled state. He immediately concluded it was unlikely she could have engaged in a blackmail scheme, but then again, maybe her apparent confusion was a clever ruse.

Cranston introduced himself as James Barrington with the Indiana District Attorney's office. He asked if she knew a Joel Dalton. Morgan affirmed that she knew him. "Barrington" explained that he wanted information about how she knew Dalton and where they first met.

Morgan replied, "Ms. Lantz told me to expect someone from the state commission on patient care. But you aren't from that agency, are you?"

"No, I'm afraid I'm not, but I am here to help you stay out of trouble, if you can help me with information about an incident you may have been involved in."

"Oh, what incident was that?" Morgan asked cautiously.

"The unexplained disappearance of Joel Dalton on June 4, 1988," Cranston stated plainly.

"Well, I, uh, have nothing to say in regards to that matter," Morgan responded nervously.

"You do know that Joel left Grassville on June 5, 1988, don't you, Ms. Morgan? What reason did he have to want to leave and permanently disappear?"

"His dad frequently beat the shit out of him and he didn't like it," she quickly replied.

"Did you help him leave? He told an associate of mine that you were supposed to pick him up at a school prom after he robbed some of the graduates."

"No, I didn't have anything to do with the robberies," Morgan stated emphatically.

"Did you drive him to Indianapolis?" Cranston asked pointedly. He sensed that Sally Morgan was getting agitated.

"No, I did not," Morgan stated emotionally.

"Were you part of the reason Joel left?"

"Okay, I paid him to leave," Morgan blurted out.

"Why would you do that? Were you covering up something bad that happened?"

"No, I was in love with Lowell Dalton, his father! But Lowell wouldn't let me move in with him, or marry him, unless Joel was out of the picture. That's why I wrote Joel a note demanding that he leave town. And I provided him enough money that he could do it."

"Alright," Cranston said softly. "Sally, I'm going to ask you one final question and then I'll leave, provided you don't lie to me. As an experienced prosecutor, I'll be able to tell if you're lying." Cranston gave her a piercing look.

He could see tension mounting in Sally. She gripped the arms of the rocking chair tightly and her eyes darted around. After a pregnant pause, Cranston asked, "Did you author another note, this one to David Weiss, asking for a great deal of money?"

"You must be out of your mind!" Morgan shrieked. "Everybody knows the Weisses are connected to the Chicago mob. I'd be crazy to risk my life threatening a Weiss. Why would I put my life on the line like that? And what the hell do you think I could do with it in here? Would I share it with the crazies that are my roommates? Hell no! I know I've got problems I need help with. I still can't live on my own..." Morgan broke off sobbing uncontrollably.

Cranston thought he'd heard enough. Sally Morgan was not capable of blackmailing anyone. He wondered why David Weiss considered her a suspect and felt threatened by her. *But that's none of my business, and some things are better left unknown.* Cranston did not want to risk putting himself in jeopardy with Weiss. The impression he'd developed of the young man through Robert Levitt was that Weiss was headstrong and was willing to take extreme measures with anyone that crossed him.

Ten minutes later, he found a pay phone and called Levitt. He shared the information he obtained from Sally Morgan. He offered the opinion that she did not have the mental capacity to threaten David Weiss or engage in a scheme to blackmail anyone. Levitt thanked him for his services, told him the job was concluded, and instructed him to send the final bill.

Levitt called Weiss and updated him with the particulars of his conversation with Edwin Cranston about Sally Morgan. Weiss replied dryly, "Well then, I guess we know who the blackmailer is." He instructed Levitt to immediately contact Jimmy Perilli and tell him to take care of things as per their prior instructions.

Chapter 25

The following Tuesday, Levitt received a mid-afternoon phone call from Jimmy Perilli. "We found him. He's hiding in a friend's basement apartment. Frankie Stenzi, a minor player in the drug business in Indianapolis, who Joel sold drugs for, took him in. Apparently, he's been at Stenzi's ever since last Sunday, when you saw him at his Indianapolis home. After your meeting with Dalton, he gave his girlfriend some money and told her to scram. And, according to Stenzi, he's scared to death of what you might do to him.

Once Stenzi found out who was interested in his friend, he contacted our associate in Indianapolis, Fred Roselli. Stenzi was paid for the information and told to be out of his house for most of the day on Wednesday. According to Stenzi, Dalton almost crapped his pants when he answered the door and saw David Weiss standing there. "Are you okay with us dealing with Stenzi ourselves?" Perilli asked Levitt.

"Yes, he's no concern of ours," Levitt stated coldly.

Well, my boss Bruno Altobello always said, "Why take

a risk if you don't have too. Stenzi has no loyalty to us and he's a minor player in the drug trade. If you don't object, I think I'll go ahead and make him disappear," Perilli replied equally coldly.

"It's your call. My boss could care less how you handle Stenzi. Now, as for Dalton, Mr. Weiss wants to meet with him again in person, contrary to my advice," Levitt said with a touch of irritation in his voice.

"Once we've nabbed him, I'll take him to a secure location out in the country. Fred Roselli owns a small farm with a secluded out-building where we'll keep him until you and Weiss arrive," Perilli stated.

"Sounds perfect, I think Mr. Weiss will be very happy with the plan."

"Roselli says nobody will be at the farm on Wednesday, but he'll be there to make sure everything goes as planned. I'll call you back with the address once I get it from Roselli," promised Perilli.

"Everything sounds well thought out. See you tomorrow," Levitt replied and then hung up.

* * *

The following morning, Jimmy and Joe Perilli surprised Joel Dalton in Frankie Stenzi's basement. Jimmy slugged him once and he passed out. They tied Joel up and placed him in a rented panel van and then delivered him to Fred Roselli's farm as instructed.

When David Weiss and Robert Levitt arrived at the farm, Roselli directed them to the out-building where Dalton awaited, tied to a chair. When Weiss and Levitt entered the building, they immediately noticed a pool of yellow liquid under the chair. Perilli said, "He pissed his pants several minutes after I told him you would be paying him another visit." Weiss stood in front of the bound Dalton staring at him. Dalton's eyes were swollen and red. It appeared that Dalton had been crying. Weiss assumed he'd been pleading for his life.

The sight of Dalton with a wrinkled, torn shirt, filthy jeans, a red and dirty face, reminded David Weiss of the Joel Dalton he knew in high school. There were stacks of old wood boxes around the perimeter of the room. Worn power tools were lined up on a work bench. A grass mower and a snow blower were next to the table. At the back of the room was an old, rusted model-A Ford covered with a tarp. Several fluorescent light fixtures hung loosely from the ceiling barely illuminating the room. Weiss walked over to Dalton and said, "When we met the other day, I really thought you'd changed, Joel. But sadly, it turns out I was wrong. Did you really think I'd pay you or anyone else blackmail money?"

Dalton sniffled and cleared his throat nervously. "I, uh, I decided to do it, but then I changed my mind and backed out. I don't want your money, Mr. Weiss. No one got hurt and I'll never tell anyone about any of this, if you let me go." Dalton's voice was desperate and pleading. "Please spare my life, I screwed up and I'm really sorry, Mr. Weiss."

David looked over to Levitt, as if the advisor was going to make the decision concerning Joel Dalton's fate. David looked at Dalton and then back to Perilli, and said looking directly into Dalton's eyes, "Why should I forgive and forget what you've done to my family and friends? My father never allowed anyone that I know of to take advantage or threaten him." Then, he looked back at Perilli and angrily said, "Give this piece of shit what he deserves."

Joel Dalton squirmed and struggled against the rope binding him to the chair. In one last desperate attempt to find some compassion in David Weiss, he pleaded, "Please Mr. Weiss don't take my life!" The last thing David Weiss heard as he and Levitt walked out of the building was Joel Dalton crying and begging for his life. Moments later, David heard three muffled shots from inside the out-building. David Weiss smiled with grim satisfaction knowing Joel Dalton was dead, as he and Robert Levitt drove off in Levitt's Mercedes.

On the way home to Grassville, Weiss looked over at Levitt and said, "Now I know what it feels like to be a gangster; no remorse and no regrets."

Levitt grunted, "I guess you do."

"Are you hungry counselor?" Weiss asked coolly.

Levitt said that he wasn't hungry and he didn't feel like eating.

Weiss ignored Levitt's response and said, "Let's have dinner at Scala Vinoteca in Bedford, shall we? I'm sure you'll be ready to eat once the aroma of their excellent food hits your nostrils. I'm really hungry and I think fresh fish at Scala Vinoteca will really hit the spot."

Levitt shot a glance over at his young boss. "Well, it is right on our way." Levitt had wondered how David would react emotionally to the execution of Joel Dalton. He sucked in his breath as he realized that he was not shocked or surprised how unemotional David was about ordering another human being's life be snuffed out. Why had David wanted to see Joel Dalton just prior to his death? Apparently to look into the eyes of the man he was going to have killed. Levitt was now sure that David Weiss was like his father, Benjamin Weiss, but decidedly worse.

After Levitt dropped off his boss at the mansion late that evening, he reflected on the events of the day during his drive home. He had trouble sleeping that night and the following morning made a decision to write a short note to David Weiss.

* * *

On Friday morning, David was going through a stack of letters on his desk. He wondered why Levitt hadn't showed up for their regular morning meeting. *He probably got caught up in a phone call,* Weiss thought. He was surprised when he discovered an envelope with a note inside on Robert Levitt's personal stationary. *Hmm, probably Robert's excuse for missing the meeting,* Weiss speculated as he glanced quickly at the note in Levitt's familiar and careful script. But then, his eyes bulged as he concentrated on the contents of the note.

Dear David:

I am officially notifying you that as of now, I'm resigning my employment with Weiss Financial. Over the years of faithful service to your father, I earned his trust and respect. It is quite obvious to me that you do not value my opinion, since you routinely fail to take my advice. And, resolving the Dalton issue didn't even earn me a simple, "Thank you."

I went to college and law school to become an attorney, and, while it's true, that I have been involved in some questionable activities in my employment with Weiss Financial, I never intended to become an accessory to an execution. On Tuesday afternoon at Roselli's farm, I'm afraid we crossed an unacceptable line, even to me.

It has been a pleasure working for Weiss Financial Group. Good bye.

Sincerely,

Robert Levitt

Attorney at Law